My Darlin' Clementine

My Darlin' Clementine

Kristiana Gregory

Holiday House / New York

Library of Congress Cataloging-in-Publication Data
Gregory, Kristiana.
My darlin' Clementine / by Kristiana Gregory. — 1st ed.
p. cm.
Summary: Expands on the folk song to tell of sixteen-year-old
Clementine, whose dream of being a doctor is complicated by her
drunken, gambling father; the lawlessness of 1866 Idaho Territory;
and the affections of handsome Boone Reno.
ISBN 978-0-8234-2198-5 (hardcover)
[1. Frontier and pioneer life—Idaho—Fiction. 2. Family life—Idaho—
Fiction. 3. Sisters—Fiction. 4. Sex role—Fiction. 5. Miners—Fiction.
6. Vigilantes—Fiction. 7. Idaho—History—19th century—Fiction.]
I. Title. II. Title: My darlin' Clementine.
PZ7.G8619My 2009
[Fic]—dc22
2008039203

For my Idaho men—
Kip, Gregory, and Cody

Oh My Darling Clementine!

In a cavern, in a canyon,
Excavating for a mine
Dwelt a miner forty-niner,
And his daughter Clementine.

[*Refrain*]: Oh my darling, oh my darling
Oh my darling, Clementine!
Thou art lost and gone forever
Dreadful sorry, Clementine.

Light she was and like a fairy,
And her shoes were number nine,
Herring boxes, without topses,
Sandals were for Clementine. [*refrain*]

Drove she ducklings to the water
Ev'ry morning just at nine,
Hit her foot against a splinter,
Fell into the foaming brine. [*refrain*]

Ruby lips above the water,
Blowing bubbles, soft and fine,
But, alas I was no swimmer,
So I lost my Clementine. [*refrain*]

How I missed her! How I missed her,
How I missed my Clementine,
But I kissed her little sister,
I forgot my Clementine. [*refrain*]

Contents

Historical Note

During the Civil War, the Boise Basin in Idaho Territory was the setting for one of the richest gold rushes in American history, said to have produced more gold than Alaska. Nugget is a fictional mining town based on Idaho City, which in 1863 had more than six thousand citizens, including hundreds of women and children. Chinese made up nearly half of the population, the highest percentage in all the Western states and territories. Some of the hurdy-gurdy girls—saloon dancers—were poor immigrants from Switzerland and Germany and as young as fifteen years old. Many managed to save their money, marry miners, and settle down to raise families.

Shooting deaths, hangings, and other violent crimes were common in mining camps. But because there weren't enough marshals, sheriffs, or deputies to catch the bad guys, justice was loose. Some historians say that Idaho City birthed the vigilante movement as frustrated citizens tried to establish a semblance of law and order. This practice eventually swept through the American West.

—*Kristiana Gregory*

PART I

Josie

Nugget

Territory of Idaho

Spring 1867

1
Wedding Day

When Pa found me standin' alone at the river's edge, he pulled me to safety.

"Josie, honey," he said, a scared look on his face, "Josie, was you here when Clementine fell in? Did you see what happened?" But I could only shake my head.

Bein' eleven years of age, it ain't possible for me to cry and talk at the same time.

He made fists at the sky and began yelling her name, but of course she didn't answer. Alls we could hear was the roar of the river. Some miners up Bear Creek who heard my screams were already searchin' up and down the banks from where I found Clementine's bridal wreath there on the footbridge. By then we were in the mountain's shadow.

Honest, for near an hour I held those yellow daisies in my hands, just starin' at the water. The bridge is narrow, that's for sure, just the flat side of a split log, but my sister and I had walked there every single day, on our way to town and back. How she fell, I can't figure.

I kept askin' God—quiet-like in my head—why He let her drown. And why of all things on her weddin' day, before even sayin' her vows? She was barely seventeen. But God didn't answer. Alls I heard was wind high up in the pines. And the river.

Poor Boone Reno was beside himself. He joined in the search, callin' for his darlin' like his heart was breakin'.

Ain't never seen a man cry before then. Boone was nineteen, but a man just the same, on account he loved my sister and wanted to be a good husband. Even built a cabin by the North Fork just for her, hopin' for a future together. It was small as a dollhouse, but with room inside for a bed and a fireplace to cook by. He showed me one night with his lantern after he had finally hung the door. Together we hammered an empty bean sack over the window to make a curtain. Oh, it was a pretty little place, but best of all, it was far enough from town so Clementine could start her new life away from Pa.

But I am off the subject.

Sunset came that terrible day sooner than any of us wanted. Men kept searchin' with torches all along the river, over boulders and fallen trees, in the eddies of pools, but no sign of Clementine. Just the river's foam showin' white in the darkness and wood smoke in the air. The only reason I knew it was suppertime was from the good smell of bacon comin' from Tall Sing's campfire. He was cookin' for everyone, trying to get us to eat.

Anyhow, Pa sat in the dirt by me, with his tin of hot coffee. He took a sip through its steam, then hung his head. Tears ran off the end of his nose. I knew he needed a kind word, but a lump in my throat kept me from talkin'. I touched his hand.

Finally he said, "Josie, honey, why was it Clementine hurried away from the chapel afore her vows, afore I got there? Did she change her mind about marryin' Reno?"

By then I had recovered my voice. "No, Pa," I said. "She just forgot somethin' from the cabin, and was comin' right back."

"What was it?"

"Don't know, Pa. Maybe Mama's handkerchief to keep in her sleeve. For sentimental reasons. She mentioned somethin' about that."

"Hmm." Pa picked up a twig and poked it into the fire. "Was she wearin' her mama's pretty brooch?"

"Reckon so, Pa. You gave it to her. It was pinned to her collar, last I saw."

Then he did somethin' that scared me. He took the twig from the fire and pointed its glowing tip at me. "Josie," he said, "what happened to our Clementine? Why'd she fall? And how come she didn't take the upper trail that's safer?" He had that same confused look as the day Ma disappeared—furious and sick with worry.

Pa had never laid a hand on me, but at that moment there was somethin' in his eyes that made me back away from him.

"Clementine's gone," is all I said before I broke down cryin'.

Early next mornin' while the sun was still behind the mountain, Tall Sing walked with me through the woods and across the footbridge to town. I kept my eyes in front of me, away from the churnin' river, nervous because the log beneath my feet was wet from its splash. Tall Sing carried my valise in one hand; his other held a pole over his shoulder with his bundle. Inside were his Chinese medicines and whatnots. We both were leavin' Nugget with every dear thing we owned.

I carried the folded-up quilt Clementine had made me. It was heavy. Nestled on top was my kitten, her green eyes lookin' up at me.

Even though Clementine was missin', Pa said I must still go live in the valley, like he and her had been plannin' for weeks. Winters would be mild, and that new little town called Boise City would be more gentle for a girl without a mother such as myself.

What he really meant was that a boardin'house lady was waitin' to take me in as a companion for her little girl. Tall Sing was to be the family cook for good pay.

Anyhow, on our way to the stagecoach I looked up at Tall Sing. His long pigtail swung behind his back as he walked beside me. "Sure am glad you're comin' with me," I told him. I took hold of his sleeve like I'd done ever since I was a baby, whenever I was scared.

His old face smiled.

In front of the bank, a team of horses was hitched to a Wells Fargo stage. Pa offered his arm to help me into the coach. I gave my father a long hug, then looked for Boone Reno. There he was, hurryin' over.

"Josie!" His voice was hoarse and he had the saddest no-sleep eyes I'd ever seen.

Oh, Boone, my heart said. He embraced me brother-like, then kissed my cheek. He nodded at Tall Sing.

As our coach headed down the trail I looked back at my sister's sweetheart and wished with all my soul that he was comin', too. My new home would be only a day away by horse-back, but I knew it would feel like an ocean separated us.

Another thing I wished with all my soul was that Pa wouldn't go completely mad now that all his loved ones were gone.

It was the last time I set eyes on Nugget, the wildest heartbreakin'est minin' town I ever set foot in.

PART II

Clementine

Nugget

Territory of Idaho

Spring 1866

2
A Thief in the Night

Cold air woke me. Pa was coming in late again, leaving the door open too long as he tried to shut it with his foot. I waited to hear him set his six-shooter on the mantel like he always did, then stir the fire. But this night was different.

I leaned up on my elbow to listen. Josie sighed next to me under our quilt and rolled over, still asleep.

Our cabin was dimly lit from coals in the grate. I could see Pa's hunched shoulders as he stooped to look under a cupboard, then under the bed he shared with Ma in their little room. If she was awake, she made no sound.

When Pa turned in our direction, he staggered and fell against the table. This frightened me. I was used to him limping on account of his aching hip, but not this bad. Since Josie and I slept in a corner, I hoped he could not see me watching him. The log wall behind us was dark, chinked with rags and mud to keep out the wind.

I smelled whiskey on his breath as he huffed and cursed—this was new, him drinking—then for some reason he crawled halfway under our bed. The boxes and tins we stored there crashed and clanged as he swept his arm along the dirt floor.

Josie gave a startled cry as she woke from the noise.

I could feel my heart beating.

By now Ma had thrown back her covers and was reaching for a lantern on her bedpost. "What's this you're up to, Dallas?" she asked him. A match flared as she held it to the wick of our oil lamp. The room blazed with light.

Pa ignored her. He knocked pans from a shelf, then spoons and tin plates. A glass jar shattered on the stones of the hearth—I could smell the honey and nutmeg of Ma's summer peaches. Next, I heard a swish as grain poured from a sack he sliced open.

Then I saw Pa's knife. The blade flashed in the lamplight like a mirror. Again my mother's voice. Softer this time.

"Dallas Kidd."

"I'll find it yet," he answered, coming back toward us. I pulled Josie into my arms and moved further into the corner. Pa stabbed at my pillow, then hers, sending feathers over us like snow falling.

At that Ma lifted the skillet off its hook and rushed up behind him. Pa must've seen her shadow because he ducked out of the way and grabbed it from her.

"Leave . . . our . . . girls . . . alone," said Ma.

Silence hung between them.

I looked down at my sister. She was under my arm, trembling. Right then she was my biggest worry. She was only ten years of age.

Finally our mother spoke. She was a slight figure in her nightgown, staring down a knife and a large iron skillet, but she did not back away from my father. "What in heavens are you looking for?" she asked. "Come now, Dallas, tell me. This is not like you."

Pa lowered the skillet to his side. He said, "Dog Face Sam is waitin' outside. We got some business to take care of."

I figured Pa had been losing at the poker tables again because Dog Face Sam owned one of the wildest saloons in town. I could not hear his name without recollecting the day of his accident—that is, the gunfight up at Cougar Creek.

Ma's gentle voice brought me back to the moment. "Right there behind you, Dallas. Under the churn. Lift it careful—"

But Pa had already kicked it over. There was a sharp smell of spilled buttermilk as he took Ma's pouch of hard-earned coins from the little hole we had dug in the dirt. All these months she'd been able to hide it from him—until now. He was gone before any of us could draw a breath, the plank door clunking shut behind him.

Odd thing was, I could tell there was more than one horse waiting on the other side of the river. Dog Face Sam must've had all his brothers with him because there were enough hooves galloping away to make up a posse.

A posse in the middle of the night meant only one thing: more trouble.

3

The Terrible Deed

Josie and I hurried to help Ma with the mess. First, I scooped up the peaches and set them outside on a rock for the racoons. If we did not clean right away, mice and wood rats could come in the night to eat our grain. By morning, ants would be everywhere in long sticky lines.

I could not tell from my mother's face what she thought about Pa taking her money or scaring us all so bad. In the lamplight she looked pretty as I'd ever seen her. Her hair was as long as mine, below her waist, so that she had to drape it over the front of her shoulder before sitting down. To think she'd swung our heavy skillet like it was just a rug beater, well, I figured Pa would be dead at our feet if she had managed to strike him.

"Ma?" I said. "What're we going to do now? Pa's getting worse." We both knew he had never pulled a knife on us before. He never started drinking till a few months ago.

She was trying to thread a needle by holding it up to the lamplight. She always took her time to answer big questions, and this night was no different. While Josie and I gathered up our goose feathers, Ma began mending the sack Pa had ripped open. One stitch, two stitch. She looked over at me.

"I am thinking on it, Clementine."

Pretty soon the hearth was mopped and all things broken swept into the fire. The feathers we would stuff into new pillows on the morrow. By the time our clock chimed half-past midnight, we had blown out the lamp and returned to bed.

I waited until I could hear the deep-sleep breathing of Ma and Josie. Then I eased my feet into the wool stockings I'd put under the covers with my cloak while we'd been cleaning up. I had wanted to warm them for what I was about to do.

I crept from bed carrying my shoes and ever so gentle opened the door, just inches wide, until I slipped outside. Quiet as a coon.

The air was frosty. While leaning against our garden fence to tie my laces, my eyes grew comfortable in the darkness. Starlight pointed down through the pine trees, reflecting off the river like fireflies. For a moment, I listened to the water washing against the banks, then I crossed the footbridge and was on my way.

We lived up Gold Digger's Canyon about a mile from the town everyone called Nugget. Our neighbors were miners mostly, camping in tents along the various creeks, but some had struck it rich enough to build a cabin in the woods for their families. I hoped to see lamplight or a friendly candle in one of their windows, but at that late hour all was dark.

* * *

Along the road I could smell droppings left behind by the horse. Here and there I bent down over a pile—my fingers just above it without touching—to feel if they were warm or stone-cold. Tall Sing had taught me this, to see if tracks were fresh without getting my hands dirty. This is how I knew Pa was headed toward Main Street.

It was long after midnight, but saloons were still aglow. Cigar smoke drifted out over their swinging doors, along with music from fiddles and pianos. As I hurried past in the shadows, I could see flashes of color from the dance girls, their dresses a-twirl with plenty of petticoat.

Where Main Street turned into the road leading out of town, my path once again was in darkness. Noise from the saloons faded behind me. I buttoned the collar of my cloak against the cold and picked up my pace to keep warm. Though it was spring, there was still plenty of snow.

Don't know what got into me that night, thinking I could spy on Pa. When I came around the bend, I wished I had stayed in the cabin with my mother and sister.

At the edge of a clearing some men—at least a dozen—were gathered around something, an animal I first thought. But then I heard someone crying, begging for mercy. Nearby were the horses, now and then jangling their reins with a restless stomp of a hoof.

Too afraid to go further, I hid behind the spreading boughs of a spruce tree and watched. Three of the men held torches that cast wobbly shadows over the group. The way they were glancing over their shoulders, well, I guessed right then that the bunch of them were up to no good.

At the edge of the circle was Dog Face Sam, tying a rope to the saddle of his horse. There was no mistaking the bulge of his broken jaw or the hole where the tip of his nose had got shot off last year. I was close enough to see the scar.

Then in the crowd I saw Pa's slouch hat, white with a dirty brim. His back was to me. I knelt low and held my breath.

"Finally got 'im for you, Judge Reno," said Pa. His voice sounded eager. "And drinks are on me when we get back to town."

"Well done, Dallas," a man replied. "It's about time. Now let's take care of this—"

Just then someone grabbed me from behind while pressing a hand over my mouth. I struggled in panic, trying to kick free.

"Shhh," a voice whispered in my ear.

I managed to twist around. Torchlight reflected off a familiar face. When I realized it was my friend Tall Sing, I nearly cried with relief. He held one finger over his lips so I would keep quiet. He was old enough to be my grandfather and, at six-feet-some-inches, he was the tallest Chinaman in town. We had known each other ever since my growing-up days in Miners Creek, and I trusted him.

He led me away from the spruce tree, my heart still pounding from him scaring me so bad. That made twice that night—being scared, that is.

From the trail I kept glancing over my shoulder, worried someone might hear the crunch of our footsteps in the snow. When we were deep in the woods, Tall Sing stopped. He was silhouetted against the starlight, looking down at me.

"Why did you follow me?" I asked him.

"You in danger."

Suddenly cheers broke out in the distance. I put my hands over my face, believing something terrible had just happened, yet what, I could not guess. I would never tell my mother that Pa had not been at the gaming tables that night, like always.

Never.

She had loved him since before I was born and loved him still. She would reckon he just stole her money to pay off another one of his debts, that's all, instead of buying a round for his friends to celebrate their villainous deed.

Tall Sing touched my arm. "Come home, Clemmy." He turned for Gold Digger's Canyon, knowing I would follow.

4
Like Nothing Happened

The moon was beginning to rise when I slipped back into the cabin and Tall Sing into his hut that leaned against our chimney. The stones there gave off enough heat so he wouldn't freeze at night and provided little ledges where he stored his medicines and herbs. I was certain he woke up when Pa had gone on his rampage and—knowing Tall Sing—had wanted to protect us.

But I knew why he stayed in the shadows. In our first mining camp—I was eight years old at the time—I saw with my own eyes that Chinamen dare not raise a hand or voice against a white man, else they be punished. Hanged from a tree without a judge or jury. Even though Tall Sing had worked for our family since the day of my birth, he took care around my father not to upset or disobey him.

He earned his wages in silence.

It seemed I lay wide awake through the long hours of that night, but suddenly sunlight was streaming in a window and Ma was at the hearth. I was surprised to see Pa in their bedroom. He must've come in during the wee hours, so I had fallen asleep after all.

Two years before, when we arrived in Nugget, Pa and Tall Sing had built our cabin in just a week. It took them five days to fell the trees, strip their branches, then lay the logs in place. They cut holes for three windows and a door, then spent two more days to heft logs up for our roof. The main room was big with a fireplace and a long table in front of it. Off to the side was Ma's iron stove and an alcove for her pantry, large enough for three walls of shelves.

Like I said before, Josie and I slept in a corner of the main room. Right away she and I had hung a blanket from one of the overhead beams so we could dress in privacy.

That morning behind the curtain I hurried out of my nightgown into my blouse, the blue one with buttons at the wrists, and my skirt. It sounds fancy, but the hem was ragged from brushing along the floor. My hair was a long tangle, so I twisted it into a braid. Even though I was sixteen, I did not like pinning it on the top of my head like other girls my age.

Now presentable, I was ready for our first customers. Ma had already started breakfast. I smelled ham frying in her skillet, the one she had threatened to hit Pa with. A basket of eggs was waiting for me to begin cracking them into the hot grease. We did not have our own chickens for these eggs, but Tall Sing went at dawn to his friends who did. He ate breakfast with them before hiking back up the canyon.

I grabbed the quilt where Josie's foot was and jiggled it to wake her.

"Time to set the table," I said.

Josie sat up fast, like she'd been awake for a while and was waiting till the last minute. She pulled the covers up to her neck, patting down the blanket and tucking one side in at the wall—her way of making our bed while staying warm. Then she crawled out the top and jumped to the floor.

A fresh bucket was by the door, another errand Tall Sing did before sunup, drawing water from the river, that is. Josie splashed her fingers in it, but instead of washing her face, she flicked the cold water at me, bending low the way puppies do when they want to play.

"I ain't goin' to school today," she said. Josie always had a smile.

"Oh, yes you are!" Ma and I said at the same instant. Then Ma added, "*Ain't* is not a word. You know better, Josie Kidd."

Josie would stay home and play all day if Ma let her. She on purpose talked like a scoundrel—sometimes with a cuss word thrown in—just to prickle our mother's high hopes for her. Ma wanted us to be proper ladies, to have the advantages she never had, but Josie wanted to be wild and dance in the saloons like the hurdy-gurdy girls. She still had not taken to book reading like I had.

I'll say this about my sister: She worked hard at her chores and liked to help.

I handed her a stack of tin plates, sixteen. Seven for along each side of the table and one for each end. Next, tin cups for coffee, then forks. We did not set out napkins on account of it being too much laundering, and besides, the men just used their sleeves or the backs of their hands.

All this was for the bachelor miners, a varied assortment who came at sunrise before trekking the rest of the way up the canyon to stand in a cold river all day. Ma was famous for her hot breakfasts—fifty cents a man. Most were placer miners, that is, they stood in the streams for hours and hours, washing their sluice boxes and pans of gravel, hoping to see a sparkle of gold. Then at sunset they would come back down the canyon for supper, ten cents each.

Ma could not bear to charge them a penny more upon seeing their tired shoulders. The men were always chilled, soaked up to their hips. Needing encouragement. Not many had found enough gold to count for anything. So, ten cents for supper. But often we would find a silver dollar under a plate when clearing the table. We figured some of the luckier men were helping the others, not wanting to embarrass them with charity, but wanting to pay Ma her due.

Anyhow, that morning Ma, Josie, and I acted like everything was regular. We talked, sure, but we did not say one word about the broken jars or feathers still scattered about. Or the knife.

If Pa recollected causing the mess, he didn't say. He sat at the edge of their bed and, real slow, pulled on his boots with swollen fingers. I could tell his hands pained him something terrible from the rheumatism. Too many years wading in icy rivers. This winter had been the worst, the cold going straight to his bones. I reckon whiskey was helping Pa not ache so bad.

When I brought him his cup of coffee, he was rubbing his sore knees.

"Morning, Papa," I said. I kissed his grizzled cheek, then drew back to look in his eyes, trying to guess what he had done the night before.

"Thank you, darlin'," he said. "Mmm, is that your ma's good breakfast I smell?"

"Yes, Papa. Your plate is ready, with extra ham like always."

I offered my hand to help him up. Pa leaned on my shoulder to take a hobbled limp. "Mornings are the hardest," he said, mostly to himself. "I'll be fine soon as I get movin'."

What had he and Dog Face Sam been up to? I wondered. *How could Pa ride a horse with his hips aching so bad? And how could his knobby fingers hold tight to the reins?*

I figured we were all pretending that morning, the four of us. Five, counting Tall Sing, but silence was expected of him as he brought in firewood. We stayed busy all right, but I did notice Ma's brow as she set platters of hotcakes in front of Pa and the other men.

She was thinking.

5
Front-Page Story

Nugget was in the nest of a valley, surrounded by forests that led up to the mountains where most of the gold was. Streams and rivers unfurled down the canyons like silver ribbons, then they split into creeks.

The prettiest to my mind was Bear Creek, which passed behind our cabin. That spring it was running high and fast from melting snows and was so icy that drinking from my cupped hand made my forehead hurt. Even so, the delicious taste made me feel happy, like a little bit of heaven was in me.

After finishing our breakfast chores that morning, Josie and I walked through the woods to the footbridge that Pa had made from the tallest tree he could find. He had split it longwise down its middle and set it across Bear Creek from one bank to another. The log's flat side was slippery from the splash of rapids and from moss growing in its cracks. On account of this, my sister and I always stepped careful. We never ran.

There was another bridge further upriver wide enough for horses, but we preferred this quicker way.

We crossed over to a quiet pool protected by boulders, and stopped to watch a mother duck with her babies. We stood real still so as not to scare them. One by one they plopped off the bank into the water and began their swim. Nearby on the beach were two white swans preening in the sun, their black beaks nibbling at their feathers. After admiring our friends for some minutes, Josie and I continued on the path to town.

Main Street was a mile long, with plank sidewalks in front of all the stores and saloons. Even early in the morning folks were about, men mostly, talking in clusters on the sunny side of the street. There was the rattle of wagons bumping over ruts and through puddles, and the noise of blacksmiths at work, their hammers clinking against iron.

From the distance came another noise, a rhythmic thud muffled by canyon walls: the stamp mills. The stamps were like iron feet marching in place—hour after hour, day and night, crushing ore carried out of the hills. The sound was so regular I hardly noticed it anymore.

Because I had passed my exams last year, only Josie went to school now. I loved escorting her through town. We had a mercantile and a meat market, a photographer's studio, cafés, banks and bakeries, a newspaper, a surgeon, a dentist, two barbers, and an assayer who weighed the gold brought in. Then to settle disputes over this gold, there were lawyers and more lawyers, enough to fill a church.

Once, just to satisfy my curiosity, I counted the whiskey shops up and down Main: thirty-three. The alleys and side streets were busy with near as many Chinese stores, Chinese gardens, and Chinese laundries. Half of Nugget's population was from across the ocean.

Along the way Josie and I paused at the open doorway of the library because it pleased me to see the arrangement of books and magazines. Its log structure was connected to the post office, but was as small as a three-seater outhouse. Our mother said such a small library was a disgrace, and it was something she intended to remedy someday. Next we passed Dog Face Sam's Saloon, Shorty's, and Lucky Jim's. Then came the brick courthouse and further still, the jail, or what we called the calaboose.

Finally we could see the schoolhouse up ahead, beyond a sunny meadow so blue with camas flowers it looked like a lake. The building was two stories high and painted red, the bell in its tower already ringing. A wild bunch of children were ignoring the bell as they played chase with a dog and yelled for the fun of it. I took Josie's hand to hurry her along.

"I'll be here to walk you home, just like regular." I gave her the lunch pail I had packed. Inside wrapped in cloth were two of Ma's hotcakes with a slice of ham in between, plus a dried fig for dessert.

My sister was always the first to wiggle out of a hug, but that morning she did not. For a moment she leaned into me, then she broke away and ran up the schoolhouse steps, two at a time. Her classroom was upstairs with the older students, forty-six last I counted.

It was crowded on account of families moving into the territory searching for prosperity. Lots of newcomers were Old Forty-niners—that's what Pa called himself—who came when the goldfields in California dried up. After all, Nugget was the biggest settlement in the Pacific Northwest, even bigger than Portland. And it was just one of the new towns carved from the mountains of Idaho, with men in need of work and their children in need of learning.

Plenty of these kids played hooky instead of going to school. Certain boys loafed around the pool halls or amused themselves by taunting the Chinese. Others crawled in the dirt underneath the saloons, prospecting in their own way—miners tipsy from too much drink were always dropping coins and nuggets through the floorboards.

But some had real jobs, such as the boy that morning on the corner selling newspapers for ten cents each—a special edition, he was shouting. Walking by, I stole a peek to read the headline.

MURDERER FINALLY BROUGHT TO JUSTICE!!!
BLACK JACK McGEE HANGED BY VIGILANTES!!!

It had happened last night. So *that's* what Tall Sing kept me from watching. A hanging.

I bought a newspaper with two nickels from my pocket. It was just one brown sheet, printed on the front like a handbill.

I read while walking to City Market.

The article said a masked robber named Black Jack McGee had murdered a Wells Fargo stage driver. Since marshals could not find him in these rough Idaho hills, vigilantes decided to help. They took matters into their own hands, even though real lawmen fussed at them for doing so.

Pa's name was not mentioned—neither was Dog Face

Sam's or his brothers—but I knew better. The report said these vigilantes were responsible for a hanging the week prior, on the road to Grizzly Camp.

A lady passing by with a lace parasol saw me reading. "Heroes," she said.

"Beg your pardon?"

"The vigilantes are heroes," she whispered, leaning toward me under her frilly shade. "Goodness knows there aren't enough sheriffs to catch all the murderers and thieves roaming these mountains. We're so much safer, don't you agree, dear?"

"Speak for yourself, ma'am." I crumpled up the paper and threw it into a nearby spittoon. *Safe* did not describe my feelings right then.

6
Double Eagles

When I crossed the footbridge I could see Tall Sing in our garden, under his wide straw hat. I gave a whistle, then he whistled back. It was our way of saying hello without talking.

The door to our cabin was open. Now that it was spring, Ma loved for the rooms to be filled with fresh air and sunlight. She smiled when I walked in.

"Hello, darlin'." She was rearranging books on our shelf, something she often did if she couldn't find time to read. At least by thumbing through the pages she didn't feel so far from civilization, she once told me.

"Someday I'll get around to reading these again," she said. "If not me, then maybe you girls will. Dear me, I do hope Josie takes to books soon."

"Me too, Ma."

My mother's braid was coiled on the top of her head like a golden crown. Josie and I were also blond, something Pa said was the prettiest gold he ever saw. He hardly talked like that lately. His bones ached from so many years standing in the creeks, and headaches made him dizzy.

Indoors at the poker table, the wind couldn't get at him. Saloons were warm and everyone knew his name: Dry Boots Kidd, called such because he no longer got his feet wet for his occupation. Sometimes he won big, but mostly he lost.

That's why Ma decided to share our table with paying customers, so our family wouldn't starve. So Dry Boots Kidd would have a warm cabin to come home to.

Ma returned a volume of poetry to the shelf, then faced me.

"Clementine, I'm going to show you something, but you must never tell a soul."

Tall Sing was still in the garden. She led me into his shed and moved aside his sleeping mat, exposing the backside of our chimney. Then she knelt on the floor and with her fingers began wiggling out one of the stones. She looked up at me, like she heard the question in my head.

"Tall Sing knows I come here," she said.

The stone out, she reached into the hole and pulled out two leather pouches. One, she showed me, jingled with double eagles, that is, twenty-dollar gold pieces. The other was filled with bits of gold that she would later take to the assayer. After sealing up her hiding place, we went outside.

It was afternoon. Pa had made us a long bench from the other half of the footbridge, which rested against the sunny side of our cabin. It was our favorite sitting and talking place. Often we went there just to listen to the river.

I had more questions.

She looked out over the creek, squinting at the brightness reflecting off the water. "Clementine, I've been setting aside a little something here and there for you and your sister. I must think of your futures. Don't know what your father will do next."

"What do you mean, Ma?"

It seemed Ma was being careful with her thoughts.

"May come a day when you girls need to take care of yourselves."

7
A Fight at School

Spring came with a burst of wildflowers, dressing up the meadows and hillsides with color. Oh, was it ever pretty. The canyon walls had bouquets in their crevices like it was the most regular thing in the world for flowers to grow from rock and patches of snow. On the breeze came songs from robins and chickadees; even a jay squawking was music to me. The wind sighed in the fir trees, and if I closed my eyes the whooshing reminded me of the ocean.

The whole world seemed friendly in spring.

There was one pine in particular that I kept my eye on. For days I watched a bluebird make her nest in a branch split open by a woodpecker's hole. Back and forth she flew, grass and twigs in her beak. When at last she settled over her eggs with a blue flash of her wing, I could not help but think of Ma.

I puzzled over what she meant by saving money for us. Now my mother and father each had a secret that I must keep to myself.

* * *

One day when I met Josie after school, she was limping almost as bad as Pa. Her hair was mussed and there was dirt on her shoulders. By her turned-down lip, I knew she wanted to cry.

"Josie, what happened?"

"Those Lester boys ain't fit for school. They're nothing but runny-nose no-accounts and oughta be in the calaboose."

"Were you fighting with them again?" I never scolded my sister about her language when she was upset.

She drew her fists to her face like a boxer ready to strike. "They made fun of Pa again, called him a lazy drunk. So I wupped Jim, the biggest boy, like this"—she punched the air—"after he pulled my braids, but then Billy grabbed my ankle and tripped me. It's cut, see?" She lifted her skirt to show me her bloodied hem.

I bent down to look. It was a deep gash, the white of her bone showing. I caught my breath. "Josie, how on earth—"

"Billy had a knife."

I swallowed hard. The Lester boys were famous for getting in trouble, so I knew who they were. Last year their mother ran away from Nugget, leaving them alone with their pa, but he was up a gulch all day. Sometimes he camped for a week at his claim while the boys stayed in town to fend for themselves. I figured the only reason they bothered going to school was on account of their teacher. She and all the other kids made the Lester boys feel like they were in a big family.

Even so, I wanted to thrash them for hurting my sister.

I sat her down at the riverbank for a better look at her wound. It was bleeding, so I untied her shoelaces and had her scoot toward the water so she could put in her bare foot. I pulled my own dress above my knees to grab hold of my petticoat—did not care if folks saw—and real quick ripped away a ruffle from my hem to use as a rag.

She gasped while I cleaned out the dirt.

"Hold still, honey," I said to her. "We got to do this right now so it won't get infected."

I worked careful as I could, splashing water on her ankle, then pressing the cotton onto the cut. After a few minutes the bleeding slowed, so I tore another strip from my petticoat and made a bandage. Tied it tight enough to stay on, but not so tight that she'd lose all feeling in her leg.

Then I helped her stand up, brushed the dirt off her shoulders. "D'you think next time you'll stay away from those boys?" I asked.

Josie answered by crossing her arms and closing her eyes. I knew that meant *Maybe, maybe not.*

"Well, then," I said, picking up her lunch pail, "come along, now. Tall Sing'll finish doctoring you up with his special medicines and you'll be fine."

We walked home slow, on account of Josie's limp. She held my hand all the way, until we had to cross the footbridge one behind the other.

8
Keeping a Secret

When Josie and I came up the path, Ma was out front on our bench, reading a newspaper in the cool sunshine. Two weeks had passed since the hanging, but our customers knew she liked to keep up on the news, so one of them had brought her a paper. And some rumors to go with it.

"Guess you heard they finally caught Black Jack McGee," she said. "Good thing, too. Those vigilantes are from Silver City and Pioneerville, the fellas at breakfast were saying. My word, Josie, why're you limping? Are you hurt?"

"Ain't nothin', Ma," said Josie. "I'll be all right."

Ma kept back her grammar correction and Josie kept back her story. If our mother knew one of the Lester boys had knifed Josie, well, it would be one more worry she didn't need.

I decided to keep Josie's secret, too.

"Mother," I said, "we're going to visit with Tall Sing. We'll be in before you start supper."

She nodded, then turned her eyes back to the newspaper.

Hmm, I wondered, as Josie and I headed for the garden, *Silver City and Pioneerville.* Whoever started that rumor did not want Ma to suspect my father.

Tall Sing unwrapped Josie's bandage, careful and slow. He took one look, then said, "Need to sew up."

He ignored Josie shaking her head and went for his medicine bag. In China, he had been a doctor, but here in America his license was no good. Most folks didn't trust how he used herbs and animal innards, or his curious treatment with needles called acupuncture. Pa, too, had been suspicious until Ma, Josie, and I came down with typhoid—I was nine years old at the time.

Pa had been so panicked he begged Tall Sing to do something, anything, to save our lives. By a miracle and some Chinese medicine, we were healed. From then on, my father shared more of his wages with Tall Sing. Said he was family and hoped he would keep living with us no matter which mining camp we settled in.

Tall Sing led us upriver, out of Ma's sight.

"Now, Josie," I said, "if you scream Ma'll hear you and come running. Do you want her to know you were fighting with the Lester boys again?"

"No."

"Do you want Pa to find out?"

"No."

"Then here, hold my hand tight and look up at the clouds."

To distract her, I pointed out a flock of geese flying overhead, then a red-winged blackbird. For some reason, I always felt hopeful hearing its liquid trill as it called to its mate.

Meantime, Tall Sing rubbed the sticky juice from a cattail plant around Josie's ankle to numb the outer skin, then cleaned the wound again, this time with whiskey. At the sting from its alcohol, Josie squeezed her eyes shut.

I watched Tall Sing thread a long fine needle. He then pricked it through the sides of Josie's skin, joining the flaps together. One stitch, two stitch. Then three, four, and five.

She near broke my hand from clamping down so hard, but she did not scream or cuss. Tall Sing tied a knot in the thread, dabbed everything with whiskey, then wrapped her ankle with a clean cloth. The stitches were in a neat dark line about an inch long.

"It's over, honey," I said. "You're the bravest girl I know."

Not until we were in bed that night and the lantern was blown out did my sister finally cry. She burrowed into the log wall of our corner, like a bluebird making a nest, then covered her face with her pillow.

I rubbed her back until she fell asleep.

That's when the craziest thought of the whole day came into my head: I wanted to be a doctor like Tall Sing.

9
Boone Reno

The first time I saw Boone Reno was the next afternoon, though at the time I did not know his name. He was on the back of a mule bucking its way across the corral. He held on to its mane, shouting and cussing for it to stop. But with a twist of its neck, the mule launched him into the air, flailing and flying, until he landed in the mud.

On account that he was lying facedown in a puddle, quiet as a corpse, I looked around for help. Only the black-smith noticed me waving, but he shrugged as if to say, *So what?*

I slipped between the rails of the fence and ran to Boone. Wasn't sure what to do, but I knew he'd drown breathing in that muddy water—that is, if he wasn't already dead.

First thing I did was roll him onto his back and give him a look-over to see if he had any broken bones. His eyes were closed. Put his head in my lap, then with my sleeve wiped the mud from his mouth. When his lips bubbled, I knew he was breathing.

"Hello?" I pleaded, patting his cheeks. "Wake up, please."

Minutes went by. The mule meantime had stopped her kicking and wandered over to us. She dropped her head to give Boone a good sniff. When he didn't move, she nudged his head with hers.

Somehow that mule breathing on Boone Reno woke him up in no time.

He squinted into the sun.

"Do you hurt?" I asked. I moved so my shadow was on his face.

He smiled up at me. "Who are you?"

Careful, I eased him out of my lap. "Saved you from drowning, that's who," I said. "You'd better get up and make sure you can walk. What were you trying to do with this mule anyhow?"

"Ride 'er." He sat up slow, turning his head left then right. "Tomorrow I got to go down the mountain to Boise City to deliver some papers to the courthouse." Then he introduced himself and explained that his father was the Honorable Judge Reno, seeing to justice in Idaho Territory.

"Hmm." I thought about the hanging and how the Honorable Judge Reno had been seeing to justice all right—but in the middle of the night.

I fetched Boone's hat from the puddle and hit it against the fence to get the water out. As I helped him stand he thanked me, keeping his arm around me while we hobbled to the stable. The mule followed us like she and Boone were friends who had merely had a misunderstanding.

When I was sure he wasn't going to topple over, I pushed his hand off my shoulder and looked square into the prettiest blue eyes I'd ever seen. He was about nineteen years old.

"If you need doctoring," I said, backing out of the doorway, "Tall Sing knows what to do. Past town, up Gold Digger's Canyon. Follow Bear Creek, then go over the bridge by Surprise Rapids."

I turned away to fetch Josie from school, wondering at myself for not telling that handsome boy my name.

Josie was in the upstairs classroom by the window that looked out over the creek.

"Just waitin' for those Lester boys to head on out," she said, answering my question before I asked it.

We left the schoolhouse, taking the long way home through town, crossing Main Street on planks of lumber laid out like a footbridge so folks wouldn't lose their shoes in the sticky mud.

Well, wouldn't you know it, somebody had lost his boot anyhow. It was planted in the mud right there in the middle of the street, surrounded by handprints like someone had gotten stuck, then crawled to safety. A sock was there, too, already trampled into a rut by horses. I figured the boot belonged to a man on account we ladies knew to stay on the walkway. Even the hurdy-gurdy girls knew better.

"Hello, Josie," a voice called.

I looked up to see my sister waving at Boone Reno. He was carrying a sack of feed to one of the wagons in front of the mercantile.

"Do you know him?" I asked.

"He's my friend."

"What?"

"We play checkers at the merc, sometimes backgammon. He's real nice, Clementine, you'd like him. He buys me a sarsaparilla or lemonade when I bring him Ma's cookies. It's a good trade. He don't have a mother, just him and his pa, the judge."

At first I was startled that my sister was friends with someone I had only met that morning, but the more I thought on it, it shouldn't have been a surprise. Josie made friends with practically everybody. Seeing as how we didn't have any brothers, well, it figured she'd find one for herself.

Boone tipped his hat and smiled. There were those blue eyes again. But I did not want any conversation, recollecting that in the stable he'd kept his arm around me longer than need be.

Josie and I kept to the sunny side of the street where it was warm, walking slow. She wasn't limping as much. I had checked her stitches that morning and was glad the wound seemed to be healing just fine. Meantime two Chinese hurried by, their slippered feet making no noise on the boards. They were carrying a large basket of vegetables between them. Friends of Tall Sing, they nodded their respects to us.

When my sister and I got as far as the saddle shop, I glanced back. Boone was lifting another sack to his shoulder, still loading the wagon. His pants were muddy, I reckoned from falling off the mule, but that is not what softened my heart for him.

His left foot was bare, not even a sock.

10
Visitor

Later that afternoon, Boone came to our cabin, but it wasn't for Tall Sing's medicine.

He was carrying an armload of wildflowers.

I noticed him from the creek where I was washing mud from my skirt. He was no longer barefoot, so I figured he must've retrieved his boot from Main Street.

Boone could not see me standing there in my petticoat, as I was hidden in the willows. Their long lacy branches hung out over the water like a curtain, and there I was, just inside, wading up to my knees. It was one of our secret places, where my sister and I went to bathe, or in summer to cool off without men staring at my legs.

While my feet grew numb from the icy water, I kept my eye on the path. Soon enough Josie was there to greet him, her hands on her hips.

"Boone," she said, "one of these days you got to take a bath and put on some clean clothes. You look poor as Job's turkey. How'd you know we live up this canyon anyhow?"

"Your sister," he said. He looked down at his pants as if seeing the mud for the first time, then handed Josie the flowers. "These are for the both of you, the prettiest girls in all of Nugget. Prettier than anyone in the whole West, far as I'm concerned."

Josie grabbed his hat off his head and put it on her own. It was a slouch hat like most of the miners wore. "Boone," she said, "you quit that flattery right now. Are you politickin' for mayor or somethin'?"

I had to bend low under the tips of the willow to see Josie and Boone as they hiked up the path toward our cabin. He grabbed back his hat and put it on.

"Not me, Josie," he said, "that would be my pa. The Honorable Judge Reno is itchin' like a pig in poison ivy to be governor of this territory."

He and my sister seated themselves on our bench, still awash with sunlight. Long shadows from the pine trees cast stripes over our roof and garden. Boone switched his hat to Josie's head, pulling it down over her eyes. I figured his being playful was how a big brother would be. She leaned back against the side of the cabin, her arms folded across her chest. I could not see her face, just her smile curving up toward the floppy brim.

"A pig in poison ivy?" she said. "Go on, I'm a-listenin'."

While they talked, I wrung out my skirt, then hung it from a branch to dry in the sun. I stepped from the pool onto the riverbank, still hidden, but able to hear every word.

"My pa would rather shake hands with a hundred strangers," Boone said, "than sit down to supper with me.

Last year he took the train to Washington, D.C., to visit President Abraham Lincoln."

"What for?" Josie asked.

"He wanted Lincoln to appoint him as the new governor for this territory," said Boone. "But Lincoln got killed before he could answer my pa. So now he's buttering up Andrew Johnson by writing letters and such—that's our new president, for your information."

"I already knew that, Boone."

Soon my skirt was dry enough to wear. I brushed the sand from my feet, tied on my shoes, then crept along the bank under a shelter of willows until I found the path only Josie and I knew about. It cut through some juniper brush, and if I ducked down and moved slow, there wasn't a soul on earth who could spot me. Blue jays and robins kept on pecking for berries and paid me no heed.

Why I took such care to hide was on two accounts.

One, I did not want Boone to discover where we bathed, and two, I did not want him to know I'd been eavesdropping.

11
An Unlikely Friendship

Josie put Boone's flowers in a jar of water, then invited him for supper. Our cabin door was open for the setting sunlight and to welcome our customers. Soon enough there were near a dozen miners wet to the knees and hungry for my mother's hot cooking.

While I helped dish up the stew I considered all that Boone had said to Josie that afternoon.

It seemed he knew that his pa and mine were fast friends but was innocent of their midnight whereabouts. He figured our fathers were just playing cards in one of the saloons. I pondered what the Honorable Judge Reno saw in Dry Boots Kidd, a man who often fell asleep under the billiard tables and borrowed money he could not repay.

My hunch was that Judge Reno liked riding wild with the vigilantes. Come daylight with his black robe on, he was real proper-like. But justice in a courtroom was slow, not quick like outdoors in the dark of night.

And my hunch about Pa was that he was finally getting

some respect, riding with heroes. Judge Reno liked men who did what he wanted.

The miners stayed long enough to have a second cup of coffee. As I cleared the plates, I noticed Boone watching me. He kept talking to the other men, but his eyes smiled at me every time I passed by. His attentions made me glad I had rinsed the mud from my skirt that afternoon and buttoned myself into a clean blouse.

By sunset our customers were leaving. I could hear the clink of coins as some of them left money under their plates. Meantime, Boone went over to Ma. She looked pretty, her face flushed from the heat of the room. Her crown of braids shone in the lamplight.

"It was nice meeting you, Mrs. Kidd," said Boone. "Thanks muchly for supper."

She handed him his hat from a row of pegs in the wall. "You're welcome, Boone," she said. "Come again. Food's hot an hour before sundown."

Just then Pa came in the doorway. He was limping, but I was relieved to see it was from his poor hip, not from whiskey. He smelled clean, like fresh air from his walk.

First thing he did was smile at Ma. He touched her forehead to move a wisp of hair from her eyes. "Evenin', Ruby June," he said, using his pet name for her. "Am late again, I'm sorry."

"Glad you're home, Dallas. I'll get you a plate." Their fingers intertwined for just long enough that Ma blushed, on account we all were watching. "Dear, we have a new guest. Boone Reno."

Pa's eyes had been lingering on Ma, but now he noticed Boone. "Why, so we do! How are you, Boone? You're the judge's boy, ain't you. Glad to make your acquaintance. I hear your pa's going to be governor." He clapped Boone's shoulder and shook hands with him. "Now there's a man's handshake, good and strong. Keep it up, son."

"How 'do, sir," answered Boone. "Well, I'll be going now. Night, Josie. Night, Clementine."

After he left, Pa said, "Well, how 'bout that? Our family's gettin' some respect. Friends with the judge's son. That's more like it."

I watched Boone take the path to our footbridge. The forest was growing dark, but overhead the sky was still light blue. Josie stood beside me.

"Ain't he sweet?" she said.

"That he is." But I was recollecting the night of the hanging, when Pa acted so eager to please Judge Reno. Now that Boone was friendly with our family, I was uneasy. What might Pa do to keep all of us in the judge's favor?

"Clementine?" Josie slipped something cold into my palm. As I closed my fingers around it I guessed it was a silver dollar. She stretched up to whisper in my ear. "Ma gave me one, too. Said we're to find our own hiding places from now on."

I thought a moment.

"I know just the spot, Josie."

12
The Test

One Saturday morning after chores, I hiked along the river below the footbridge to see the swans. For an hour I watched as they drifted in the pool, never more than a few inches apart. Don't know why, but I found comfort in their togetherness.

This was one of my favorite places. It was tucked between high canyon walls, quiet from the pounding stamp mills. Besides the birds that flew there to swim, there was another curiosity: A cloud of steam hung over the pool like fog. When I had first noticed it—while Tall Sing and Pa were building our cabin—I stepped careful around the rocks until I discovered a hot spring bubbling up from the earth.

That's where I was when Tall Sing came down the path leading Josie by the hand, grandfather-like.

"Clemmy," he said. "You do."

I looked up. "Do what?"

Josie crossed her arms like she did when being stubborn.

"These stitches got to come out," she said, "today. Else my skin'll grow a lump there. That's what Tall Sing says, anyhow."

I regarded his face as he squatted on the ground. His long pigtail hung down his back, almost touching the sand. He handed me a cloth bundle wrapped in string.

"You do," he said again.

I untied the string, then unrolled the cloth. It was blue cotton, the same as his smock. Inside, dry and clean, were some of his medical tools, needles and such. The other day I had confided in him my dream of doctoring, but suddenly I felt jittery.

"It's okay, Clemmy," he said. "You want to be doctor. Time to start is now."

I closed my eyes to collect myself, then looked at my sister. She had seated herself on the riverbank between us, her leg stretched out and her hem drawn above her ankle so I could examine her.

Good, I thought, *no redness, no swelling.*

First I washed my hands in the creek, then shook them in the air to dry. On the cloth was a pair of scissors. I picked them up, leaning close to Josie's foot. Careful as could be, I cut the knot at the edge of her stitches. Then toward the other end, I eased the sharp point between her skin and the thread to cut there, too.

Josie squirmed.

"Hold on, honey," I said.

After I returned the scissors to the cloth, I used tweezers to pull out the black threads. By the time Josie sucked in her breath, I was done.

Tall Sing's old face creased. He nodded his approval.

Well, if a heart could soar, mine surely did at that

moment. Removing Josie's stitches was only a taste of doctoring, but it made me feel alive.

Turns out, Tall Sing had another test for me.

While Josie was at the mercantile playing checkers with one of her classmates, Tall Sing took me to the alley behind Shorty's Saloon and up the stairway. Inside it was dark and smoky. He walked to the end of a hallway, rapped twice on a door, then went in.

Two women were sitting in chairs on either side of a bed. The room was cold and there were no windows to let in the sunlight. The only heat was from an oil lamp on a bureau. My throat began to tighten at the odor of rotten meat. It was so foul I worried my breakfast might come up.

Tall Sing spoke to them in a low voice. Then he stood over the patient, pulling back the covers.

A man lay there, eyes closed. Wrapped around his chest was a bandage, stained black with blood. Tall Sing set out his instruments on a low table. He worked slow and careful to cut away the strips of cloth. When I saw three holes by the man's bare ribs, I figured he had been shot. Last man I saw so tore up by gunfire was Dog Face Sam.

Wanting to help Tall Sing, I moved close enough to hand him some tweezers, different from the ones I used on Josie. These tips were long and angled.

As he probed the wounds, the wet sound and the smell of blood made me feel sick. I swallowed hard, trying to think of the man's misery instead of my own, though at the moment it appeared he was either dead or out cold.

When I noticed Tall Sing squinting, I quick reached for the lamp to turn up the wick. In an instant, golden light moved up the walls, brightening the room so he could see better.

And soon enough, he was washing his hands in a bowl, with water one of the ladies poured from a pitcher. He then gave her some packets of medicine in folded squares of paper. In return, she gave him a small pouch jingling with coins.

On the bureau was a china bowl holding the three misshapen bullets.

I was still fighting for my stomach when we stepped outside into the fresh air. I took a deep breath. From the top of the stairway I could see down to the shaded alleys, muddy with melting snow. Some boys were chasing a dog up a side street, yelling for it to come back. Like always, Main Street had a parade of wagons and horses. The sidewalks were crowded with miners and mountain men shopping for supplies, Chinese under their flared hats, and ladies holding the hands of small children.

I took another deep breath.

Just a regular day for most folks, I thought.

Tall Sing rested his hand on my shoulder, then headed down the stairs. It was time to fetch Josie.

Only then did I notice my hands were shaking.

13
Josie's Report

Like the coins Josie and I hid away, I decided to also hide my dream of doctoring from Pa and the others.

It started this way:

At supper that night, our customers were making their regular conversation. This meant teasing Josie and flattering the both of us. The men were good-natured, but I wanted to coax them away from their favorite game, which was trying to get me to pick one of them for a husband.

"What's the news today?" I asked, to change the subject. I never mentioned gold or asked if they had discovered any in their pans that day. Never.

Well, before any of the men could answer, Josie blurted out a report on the Lester brothers. Since her wound was healed, she must've figured it was safe to mention it in front of our mother.

"And guess who took out my stitches?" She lifted her chin to regard the miners seated around us. But before anyone could answer *that* question, she said, "Clementine, that's who."

A log in the fireplace snapped as it settled into the coals. The room suddenly felt too warm. I quick looked at Ma to see her reaction. Her brows were knit together with her own questions, which I figured had more to do with Josie's fighting than with me using medical scissors.

One of the men said, "Well, well, what d'you know? Reckon we'll be calling her Doc Clementine someday."

Meantime Pa had limped through the door and shut it with his elbow. He seated himself at the table, at the empty spot Ma always saved for him. But this time he was liquored up. I could tell by the way he waved his spoon in the air.

"Doctor!" he cried. "Who's the fool that said that?"

Our customers fell silent. And I did, too, figuring it was not the moment to tell about being upstairs at Shorty's Saloon that morning. But Pa was roaring mad now, embarrassing those of us who loved him.

"Doctorin' is man's work," he said. "Everyone knows that. Girls have their duties, we have ours."

I shrank inside myself—but only for a moment—then some kind of gumption rose up.

"Pa," I said, while pouring the men coffee, "there was a lady doctor up to Wagon Creek Camp last summer. I read about her in the newspaper."

"Ha! Well, those fools in Wagon Creek better hope they never get sick."

"Why's that, Papa? Why?"

Pa's spoon was still in the air. He was trying to put his words together. "Females are weak," he answered. "They scare easy. Ever see a man cry over a dead kitten? Course not."

I walked over to him and plunked his coffee cup down with a splash. "What's wrong with crying over a dead kitten, Papa? And what's wrong with being scared? Last summer when Ma faced down that grizzly with her rifle, she was scared, but did it matter one bit?"

Pa's mouth dropped open. He looked up at me, shocked by my sass.

Meantime, one of the men everyone called Whiskey Nose was glaring at him. He was a regular customer and not afraid of my father on account he, too, drank enough to stay agitated.

"Dallas," he said, "see this?" He held up a stump of his arm. "It's what's left of my fight at Gettysburg, and guess what? A lady doctor operated on me better'n any man could have, 'cause she had a heart as big as the Rockies. Know what else, Dallas Kidd? There's a college 'specially for girls to be doctors, back east in Pennsylvania. That's where she graduated, told me herself. So what d'you think about them apples?"

Well, Pa got heated up over that, so he and Whiskey Nose started arguing. They got so loud Ma went over to Pa and real gentle took his elbow and led him to the door. Cold air rushed in as he went out, Whiskey Nose at his side, the two of them making an unholy noise like a pair of crows.

Upon their exit, peace returned to our supper table, where conversation picked right back up without anyone blinking. Josie began filling in her story with more details—made up some new ones, too—even demonstrating her punch to the oldest Lester boy.

But I stayed quiet, thinking on what Whiskey Nose had said, wondering where Pennsylvania was.

14
A New Duty

Spring passed, then it was June. Snow still clung to the hill-sides that faced north and along the shady side of the river. As most animals were out of their dens and enjoying the longer days, we could observe them going about their business.

I particularly favored the yellow-bellied marmots that darted among the rocks by our cabin, calling to one another with their loud chirps. Our name for them was whistle pigs, and they seemed as happy to be outside as my sister, now that school was over.

"Hoo-ray, Hen-ry," she said. "Us kids got to have a chance to daydream."

"Well and good," Ma answered, "but summer's no excuse for our minds to be idle."

So Ma sent us to the library every time we went to town, to see what magazines or books were brought in by stage. Like I said before, the library wasn't much bigger than a fancy outhouse, but Josie and I could stand in there together to look at the shelves. She still wasn't keen on reading, but she did love to hear a story told.

We wrote our names on a slip of paper nailed to the wall, with the titles we were borrowing—this time an issue of *Harper's Weekly*, three months old, and a novel called *Alice's Adventures in Wonderland*—then put them in our basket to finish our errands.

"So long, girls," said the librarian, who was, of all people, Whiskey Nose. On account of his bad luck with mining and his only having one arm, he worked in town. The people of Nugget paid him to keep the library open and also to run the post office next door. Like Pa, he was gentle and sweet when sober.

"Say hello to your mother," he said from behind the counter. His eyes then returned to the open book in front of him: *Poems of True Love,* his finger moving across the page with each word he read.

"Yes sir," I said. "See you at supper."

The sidewalk was crowded with ladies in hoop skirts and men talking to one another. Unsupervised children ran among the hitching posts, stirring up as much dust and noise as the horses. Around the corner, a Chinese man was painting a sign on the window of his restaurant, his door open to an aroma that made me hungry again. Meantime, the boards thumped under our footsteps, time and again popping up a nail like a marmot from its hole. That is how we came upon Boone Reno.

He was in front of the bakery. Hammer in hand, he was tightening the loose boards, going up one side of Main Street then down the other. When he saw us, he stood up and took off his hat.

"Afternoon, ladies. How 'do?"

"Fine and dandy," I answered. Then, feeling bold, I invited him to supper.

His blue eyes crinkled with his smile. "Don't mind if I do, Miss Clementine."

"Good," I said. "You can sit by Whiskey Nose."

On the way home I wanted to tell Josie about the man with three bullet holes in his chest and how good it made me feel to be a part of his healing. He had given such a look of gratitude when I removed his stitches—well, I would never forget it.

Then a few days later, Tall Sing had taken me to another saloon. It had become our secret, me helping him when Pa was out gambling or drinking. We went upstairs, where a lady was in childbirth. I wanted to tell Josie about that, too, what a miracle it was to see a baby being born. But my sister liked to tell stories so much—especially other people's—that I worried she would repeat it at the wrong time in front of the wrong audience. Namely Pa.

I did not want him to send Tall Sing away. He could and he would if he thought my learning medicine was keeping me from an important duty. Such as the one he told me about at breakfast that morning.

"Clementine," Pa had said, stirring cream into his coffee, "you'll make a good wife, and the sooner the better."

I stared at him. "*What?*"

"You're sixteen, sweetheart. It's time you had a husband who'll take care of you. My bride—your own beautiful mother—was still in her teens when we made our first home there in Californie."

Eight miners who had just begun cutting their hotcakes with their forks stopped to look at my father. Were they hoping he meant one of them?

"I don't need taking care of, Papa."

Now the miners turned their heads to look at *me*. I knew from past conversations and compliments that any one of them would be happy to have my affection.

Pa regarded me with tenderness, a look that always made me go soft. I did not want to fight with him. Especially not in front of our customers, who were watching us, silent as stones. Suddenly Pa's face cringed with pain and he began rubbing his wrist. It was the one Ma said hurt the worst.

After a moment, he said, "Alls I want is for you to be happy, Clementine. On that account, I've been wrestlin' with some ideas."

"What kind of ideas?" I asked.

The miners watching me now turned back to Pa.

I, too, looked at him, wondering. It was morning and so far the only thing he'd been drinking was Ma's strong coffee—meaning he was sober. But still he didn't answer.

Maybe it was the rheumatism that kept him quiet for the rest of breakfast. Or maybe, like Ma, he was thinking on things.

15
Plenty of Thoughts

When Josie and I got home, we wiped dishes, and I pondered Pa's announcement. Marriage had been a faraway thought, but now it settled on me like an unwelcome cloud. Right then, I resolved to distract Pa from the subject for as long as possible.

Meantime, it was Josie's day to help Tall Sing in the garden, and mine to pick huckleberries with Ma. I was glad for a chance to be alone with my mother.

We saddled the horses, then headed up the canyon. The sun was so hot, I soon tasted salt on my lips. And soon too, our mares began tossing their heads, like they sensed danger. Mine began to quiver, and when she started panting, I knew she was on the verge of a wild run.

"Shhh," I said, leaning forward to pat her neck. The whites of her eyes showed as she stepped backward, trying to turn for home. I wrapped the reins around my hands, and pulled hard to stop her from bolting.

Up ahead the trail curved toward a meadow. And sure

enough, there was a grizzly with two cubs. The mother was huge with a humped neck. It was our good fortune to be downwind where they couldn't smell us, but we caught a whiff of them. A rank, musky odor.

I held the reins tight, trying to keep my horse quiet. When some twigs cracked under her hooves, the grizzly swung her big head toward us and stood up on her hind legs, like a man in a fur coat. Her jaws opened with a growl that made my skin prickle. One enormous paw swiped the air. Its claws were curved and as long as my fingers.

Though we were hidden in the trees, I was nervous. Ma did not have her rifle like last summer.

We knew about the ferocious grizzly, how fast they ran, and that they climbed trees to get at a human. A female with her young was the most dangerous of all. A few weeks ago, a mountain man named Wild Joe came for supper. When he took off his hat, I near dropped the pot of beans I'd been spooning out. He was missing the left side of his scalp and his entire ear.

"Grizz got me," he told us. All during our meal, he described the gruesome attack.

Well, that's all I could think of right then: Wild Joe with no ear. And us with no weapon.

There was nothing for Ma and me to do except wait. The grizzly dropped to all fours and led her cubs further up the trail. After some minutes, they ambled across the meadow into brush that footed the hillside. We waited until the leaves had stopped rustling with their passage, then resumed our search for berries.

I was in a talking mood. "Ma, I do not like what Pa said at breakfast this morning."

"Now, Clementine, you're a strong girl. Smart, too. If you have dreams for yourself different than Pa's, well, you stick to them."

Something else was on my mind. "How far away is Pennsylvania?" I asked.

At this, my mother smiled. "My darlin' Clementine, I am going to sit you down with my atlas. It's time you study what's east of the Mississippi."

We continued up the trail to an elbow of Dead Eye Creek where there were clusters of miners. They stood knee-deep with their pans and stooped shoulders. Many of them were Chinese. As we passed by, each man glanced up at us, curious, then went back to his work. We recognized several from our table.

Will Pa choose one of our customers? I wondered. He liked the idea of striking it rich, so it figured he might want me to marry a prospector. An American prospector, that is.

For every few berries I picked, I ate one. Couldn't help myself, they were so delicious and thirst satisfying. Meantime, Ma and I kept an alert eye, watching for bears. When at last our buckets were full, we hung them over our saddles and headed for home. Our fingers and lips were stained purple with their sweet juice, our hands scratched from the thornbushes that grew around them. I liked how it felt to be outside all day in the fresh air, my cheeks sunburned.

Our trail went along the river. For a long stretch, the roar of rapids drowned out our voices. Then with a sudden hush the water flattened as it flowed over deep pools, quiet and speckled with trout. I again complained about Pa wanting to find me a husband.

Ma's saddle creaked when she leaned over to put her hand on mine, like she always did to soften my worries. "Clementine, don't be afraid to pursue your dreams," she said again.

It seemed Ma understood why I was asking about Pennsylvania.

16
Shorty's Saloon

That night, I decided to follow Pa when he slipped out of the cabin.

I had been in bed watching the firelight, unable to sleep, still troubled by his plans for me, so when I saw his shadow and heard him lift the latch on our door, I was already awake. It took only a moment to find my shoes, tuck the blanket around Josie, then step outside. A glance at our clock told me it was ten minutes to ten.

It was foolhardy, but I hoped to protect my father from danger—if a daughter could even do such a thing.

Summer nights are cold in the mountains, so I was glad for my shawl. Pa was careful across the footbridge, as was I. By the light of a half-moon I trailed him down the canyon into town. He limped along at a good pace.

At Shorty's Saloon he pushed through the swinging doors. I stayed outside by the hitching post, petting the horses tied up there, hidden behind their tall backs. I'd never been in the saloon itself, just upstairs with Tall Sing. Even from the sidewalk I could smell the stink of cigars and hear men shouting.

Ma had warned me forever-and-a-day not to ever, ever set foot in a place such as this, where miners might be wild with drink and not caring about the morrow.

But I was going in anyway.

At the entrance I barely missed stepping in a large, yellow puddle. Then when my foot touched a splatter of vomit I reconsidered Ma's advice. I decided to just look in a window.

Much of the noise came from a piano man banging out a tune that had the hurdy-gurdy girls waving their skirts in a scandalous manner, as Ma would put it. Their young faces surprised me—they seemed to be about my age. I wondered who they were and why they lived in Nugget.

A different sort of lady, older with bright orange hair, was at one of the tables. She wore a low-cut satin dress and was dealing a deck of cards. Her lips and cheeks were painted red, but her eyes were dark. She slapped down a card, then leaned over to spit a gob of something onto the floor.

Just then a crack of gunfire came from inside, silencing the crowd. It startled me plenty, but quick as you can rewind a music box, the piano man went back to work and the dancing continued. Conversations picked right up. The bullet had smashed a hanging lantern, but otherwise did not seem to bother anyone.

But where had my father gone?

I ran to the end of the block and around the corner. Then

I crept over to the saloon's back window to look for him there.

Pa was not on the dance floor or at any of the poker games. Couldn't see him at the long oak bar where twenty or so miners were propped on their elbows. Since Shorty was the proprietor, he was behind the bar wiping it with a rag. Like his name, he was short, but he wore high-heeled boots so he could see over the counter. His dark hair fell to his shoulders. The mirror above his shelf of bottles reflected the holster strapped around his apron and his ivory-handled pistols.

Shorty was one of Ma's favorite customers on account that he was always sober and upon occasion quoted Shakespeare. He came every breakfast and supper, closing the saloon for those few hours. Ma and I liked to speculate about his literary upbringing and why he ended up in a mining camp.

Much as he and I were friendly, he would have been disappointed to see me in his establishment. Another reason I was glad not to have gone in.

Still standing outside, I felt someone behind me.

"Evenin', pretty gal." The voice was at my ear, a faceful of whiskers prickling my cheek. Whoever it was stunk to high heaven. I shoved him away.

In the dim light I recognized Jesse Blue, one of Pa's old friends from California who often came for supper. He was straightening his suspenders, I reckoned from having just visited the outhouse. I did not like the way he looked at me right then, with a sleepy-eyed wink. It wasn't proper.

"Have you seen my pa?" I asked him.

Instead of answering, he put his arm around my waist. But real quick I peeled away his fingers and stepped aside. "Keep your distance, Jesse Blue. I'm here looking for my pa."

Still gazing at me too friendly, he pointed to a nearby corral. "Went thataway. Him and LeRoy. Ah, why won't you dance with me, Miss Clementine?"

"You mean LeRoy Reno? Judge Reno?"

"Yep."

My heart sank.

I ran up the alley. Squinting into the darkness, I could see horses leaving through the wooden gate, their dark shapes lit by torches.

I caught sight of Pa's silhouette as he climbed into his saddle. I thought to call his name, but stopped myself. Would his daughter shouting like a saloon girl makes things better for him or worse?

Dog Face Sam was on his horse, unaware that I was leaning against a dark fence, close enough to smell how bad he needed a bath. I puzzled over a clicking sound coming from his hands. When I saw what it was, a chill went through me. He was twirling the chamber of his revolver, loading it with bullets.

Then came the voice of Judge Reno. "Where are you, Dallas? We need you."

"Over here, Judge," Pa called. "Ready to go. I'm your man."

"Glad you're with us again, Dallas Kidd!" yelled another voice.

"Then let's get outta here!" someone shouted. A burst of thundering hooves filled the air with dust. The horsemen rode into the darkness, their torches small bouncing lights.

There was going to be trouble, I just knew it.

Turns out, Pa was not my biggest worry that night.

When I crossed the alley heading for home, who should I see on the other side of the street? There in a saloon window was one of the dancing girls I'd seen around town.

And with her, happy as you please, was my sister Josie.

17
The Audition

By the time I had darted around the muddy ruts of Main Street over to the sidewalk, I was plenty mad. I stormed into the saloon, grabbed Josie by the arm, and hauled her outside.

"Josie Kidd"—I paused to catch my breath—"what in blazes are you doing out this late hour? If Ma wakes up she'll be beside herself with all of us missing."

"Well, I wondered where you'd gone to, and besides—"

"That's no excuse. You're just ten. It's dangerous for a girl to be out in the middle of the night." As those words came out of my mouth I recalled that I too was guilty of being in the woods by myself, and not just once. A terror I didn't want to remind her about right then was all the abandoned mine shafts. The hills were pocked with them. One misstep and my sister—or I—could vanish, never to be seen again.

I turned my attention to her companion, who had come outside. She had braids like my sister and wore a long cape over her dress. "How old are you?" I asked.

"Fourteen."

"Fourteen?" I looked through the saloon window where we were standing. Inside it was crowded like Shorty's, the same noise and haze of cigar smoke. "You work in there?"

She glanced at Josie before answering. "We're putting on a play next month, and we need another actress."

Oh no, I thought. *More trouble.*

"What's your name?" I asked.

"Penelope."

"Penelope, does your ma or pa know where you are right now?"

She looked down at her shadow stretching across the boards. Only then did I notice that her high-buttoned shoes were worn through at the toes and weren't buttoned at all, but instead fastened around the ankle with rope. Her dress came to her shins, like she'd grown out of it long ago.

I waited for her to explain, meanwhile catching the eye of my sister.

Josie was mouthing a word. It took a moment before I understood she was saying "orphan." Then she said aloud, "Penny lives upstairs here with her aunt."

The girls waited for me to say something. All I could think of right then was that Penelope was a bad influence on my sister. Josie did not need a friend who was free to come and go at any hour, especially one who worked in a dance hall.

"Penelope, I'm sorry but—"

Josie broke away from me. "Ain't fair, Clementine."

I sighed.

"The role is *perfect* for me," she said. "It's a vaudeville. I'll get to sing *and* dance."

"Josie—"

"But I already auditioned."

"You did? When?"

My sister crossed her arms with her look of determination. "Half an hour ago."

"And Josie got the part," said Penelope. Even in the shadows I saw them smile at each other. I could tell by my sister's eager look that she admired this older girl.

My heart softened at Penelope's ragged appearance, and I made a decision. "Won't you come to supper tomorrow night?" I asked.

She drew in a breath of surprise. "Oh yes, thank you very much."

We were distracted by gunshots down the street and shouts. A group of men poured out of a saloon, followed by a woman who began screaming. Her cries scared me. Someone had just been murdered, I was sure of it. I took Josie's arm.

"Time to go," I said. "Penelope, you best get inside too, where it's safe. The sheriff's not in town this week, so no telling what those folks are going to do."

As Josie and I hurried up Gold Digger's Canyon, following a thread of moonlight, I wondered if I had handled things all right. It seemed to me that if Ma could welcome the likes of Whiskey Nose and Jesse Blue, she wouldn't think twice about sharing our table with a dance hall girl.

18

A Waiting Light

Just as Josie and I approached the footbridge, we saw a lantern on the other side of the river. Someone was hurrying our way. As the speckled light swung out in an arc I realized it was our mother, her skirt flaring with her stride.

She was calling our names, panic in her voice.

"Here, Ma," I cried. "We're coming!"

Ma held her lantern high to throw light across the bridge. "Take it slow," she cautioned.

Josie and I inched along the damp log. Water splashed our feet. I made her go in front of me so if she slipped I could grab her in time. All the while I felt ashamed. Ma would be upset with me, the oldest sister out too late, setting a poor example for Josie.

But I dared not report about Pa. I was scared for him, and for my mother, too. Would she leave Pa if he was up to no good? For now, it seemed I should tell her only part of the story.

I did not like having so many secrets.

When we had safely crossed the river, Ma set her lantern in the dirt and pulled us both into her arms. She didn't ask where we were or why, but I wanted to give some explanation, an apology for upsetting her.

"Ma," I said, her arm still around me, "I couldn't sleep—"

"Me neither," interrupted Josie. "Ma, I followed Clementine without her knowing. She didn't have nothin' to do with it and she's already scolded me so you don't have to." She threw her thin arms around Ma's neck with a sorry-as-ever hug. "I won't never do it again, Mama, promise."

The metal handle of Ma's lantern squeaked when she picked it up. She held it toward the dark path in front of us, then out on all sides. We were surrounded by forest, tall black trees alive with the sounds of night creatures. Overhead the sky had darkened, the half-moon now out of sight. The bravery I had felt earlier was gone. I was glad for Ma and her lamp.

As if hearing my thoughts, Ma said, "Girls, there's a cougar—a mountain lion—real close. Found its prints when I left the cabin a few minutes ago. Thank God it didn't track either of you. Let's hurry now."

While Josie and I settled under our quilt, Ma blew out the candles. I figured to tell her at breakfast about my sister's audition, and about our new dinner guest.

A nearby rustling startled me. Josie was already asleep so I stayed still, not wanting to wake her. Held my breath until I knew the noise was coming from outside, on the other side of our wall. Something was sniffing at a tiny space between the logs. I put my eye against the wood, but could not see in the darkness what it was.

My first suspicion was the family of raccoons that came out at night, looking for food we'd left on the rock for them. But this creature was bigger than a raccoon, its steps heavy as it paced back and forth. I sat up to look for our rifle. In the firelight I saw its long shape over the doorway, resting on the hooks of two antlers. Pa had taught me how to hit a bull's-eye and—thinking about the animal out there—I would not hesitate to shoot if we were in danger.

My thoughts turned to Pa, who might be coming up the path at this late hour, guided only by starlight. If a cougar was waiting for him, how would I be able to find either of them in the darkness? By accident I might shoot my father.

This troubled me. But just when I was about to get out of bed for the rifle, the noise outside stopped. I put my ear to the wall to listen. No sniffing, no footsteps. Reckoning the visitor had left, I lay back down.

Soon my mind grew fuzzy and, too tired to keep worrying, I closed my eyes.

By sunup, Pa hadn't come home yet.

19
Rattlesnake Station

That morning at breakfast our customers were unusually quiet. No one asked to Pa's whereabouts. Ma held her head high as if everything was regular, but Josie and I looked at each other.

Something wasn't right. I feared the mountain lion had been lying in wait for our father, but I kept that worry to myself.

"We're going to the library," I told Ma after we'd swept the floor.

"Josie," said Ma, as we hung up our aprons, "I'll be glad to meet your new friend at supper. But you will not be in a play with her, nor will you be dancing in a saloon. Is that clear?" Ma's firm voice meant there was to be no argument.

"Yes, Mama," Josie replied.

Even though the sun was hot, our path through the forest was cool. Tall Sing came with us. He whistled to the marmots that were playing among the rocks. Some of them stopped and sat on their haunches like puppies, cocking their heads to see who was calling. Josie laughed out loud at this game. Last year she found one of their babies and kept it in her pocket for an entire afternoon. But by the time she had brought it home to show Ma, the poor thing had suffocated. Now she was content to watch them from a distance.

On our walk to town, Tall Sing carried a pole over his shoulders, a basket on each end. Inside were our dirty linens and clothes. We weren't rich folks, but on account of all the Chinese laundries in Nugget, Ma was glad to pay them and Tall Sing with her earnings. No longer did my sister and I have to work a whole day washing. Tall Sing would drop off the baskets at his friends', then by the following afternoon everything would be clean—hung out in the fresh air to dry, ironed with potato starch, folded into neat stacks, and delivered to our doorstep.

Like I said, we weren't rich, but sometimes I surely did feel so.

On our way I was watchful in the woods, without confiding my worries to Tall Sing or my sister. I looked for signs of Pa, footprints in the dirt or broken branches, something that might show he had tried to come home last night.

But everything looked regular. The ducks were at the pond, also the two swans. There was only the chittering of squirrels and songbirds. Yellow-bellied marmots were so numerous, their whistles escorted us all the way down the rocky canyon.

At Main Street we went our separate ways, Tall Sing up Hap Wo Alley, Josie and me continuing to the library. A Wells

Fargo stage had just pulled up next door, in front of the post office. Some boys had unharnessed the team and were leading it down the block to the livery stable, dust kicking up under the many hooves. There were only five horses instead of eight.

A crowd waited outside in the sun, many of them Chinese, some in cone-shaped hats. All were looking up at the driver, who stood on top of the coach. A bloody sling was around his arm and he moved slow, like he was hurting. With his knee he rolled sacks of mail to the edge of the roof, then let them drop to the ground. The luggage he also pushed to the edge, toward hands reaching up to help.

As he did this, folks were calling questions to him.

I moved closer to listen, Josie at my side.

". . . Rattlesnake Station," the driver answered. "Same robbers as last week, them that took a chest of gold bars. This time alls they managed was to cut loose three of my horses before I got off a shot, kilt one of 'em. Blasted 'im out of his saddle. The posse's after the gang right now—"

"You mean Reno and his boys?" a man shouted.

"Yep."

A miner standing next to me took off his hat and waved it in the air. "Hoo-ray for the vigilantes!" he yelled.

My insides twisted. Rattlesnake Station was on the Oregon Trail, at least a day's ride away. No telling where the robbers were now. Probably hiding in the hills with their rifles and six-shooters. Aiming for whoever would try to capture them.

What made my stomach sick was that Pa was just Dry Boots Kidd, a near cripple from the rheumatism. It wasn't like him, this rough riding with guns. All because he wanted Judge Reno to like him, he was going wild.

My sister's curiosity as to Pa's whereabouts went only so far. This morning she had speculated he was probably just sleeping it off in one of the saloons and would come home later with a headache. She had the good habit of assuming the best of our father. I wished I could still do the same.

Both doors to the post office and library were closed and there was no sign of Whiskey Nose. Now *that* puzzled me. Sure, he drank too much and sometimes he cried when Ma told him supper was over and it was time to go home, but he was so glad for his job he never missed a day. Everyone could count on him. With only one arm, he managed to sort the mail just fine, and he could shelve books in proper order. Good ol' Whiskey Nose.

I cupped my hands to peer in a window. To my surprise he *was* inside, asleep on the floor with a blanket pulled up to his chin. While the crowd was still questioning the driver, I let Josie and me in the door, closing it behind us.

Whiskey Nose didn't respond to us calling his name, so I shook his shoulder to wake him. I thought it curious that his blanket was soggy. It felt sticky. I backed away, and that's when Josie screamed.

My hand was covered with blood.

20
A New Postmistress

According to the doctor summoned from his fried eggs and coffee, Whiskey Nose was alive, but barely. Two men made a stretcher from their jackets tied together and hauled him upstairs at Shorty's, blood getting all over their shirts. Josie and I ran after them, but were told to stay on the sidewalk.

"Doc has things under control," said a barber, his hands in the air to stop us. "Go about your business now, girls."

That made me mad. Sure, I was no doctor, but Whiskey Nose was our friend and maybe we could at least comfort him. He'd woken up long enough to say my name and ask for a sip of water.

Folks were all a-talk about what might have happened. The post office was strewn with letters and torn-up paper. Robbery some said, and Whiskey Nose with only one arm couldn't stop it. Got stabbed for trying. Then to hide the crime, someone laid him out like he was sleeping.

To my mind, it was peculiar for a thief to cover his victim with a blanket.

Meantime, I figured one way to help Whiskey Nose was to clean up the mess. Josie and I returned to the post office and sorted through the disarray until we could make sense of what was what. We swept enough dirt from the floor to fill a flowerpot.

When I noticed three sacks of mail were still outside, with folks rooting through them for their letters and such, I said a bold thing, which at first was a falsehood, but then turned out to be true.

Boosting myself up onto the rain barrel, I stood on its rim to be taller. "Excuse me," I said.

No one noticed.

"Excuse me!" I said again, louder.

A few faces turned my way. From up high I could see that the women had left, and many of the Chinese were turning away. Most of them wore dark blue smocks, but a few were dressed like miners—in plaid shirts and slouch hats. One thing they each had in common, though, was a single pigtail hanging down to his waist. I hoped they would come back. I reckoned they might be expecting packages from San Francisco, like Tall Sing often did.

"Gentlemen!" I finally yelled. "There's been a stabbing of bloody proportions!" Instantly, the crowd looked up, murmuring questions. I explained about Whiskey Nose.

"Meantime, folks," I went on, "I'm Clementine Kidd, your new postmistress until Whiskey Nose gets better. My assistant and I"—here I glanced down at Josie, hoping she was willing—"we'll organize your mail and get the library situated with the new magazines and books that just arrived by stage. Come back tomorrow, please."

At that I jumped down from the barrel. But being distracted and upset about Whiskey Nose, I forgot to grab my skirt. My feet landed fine, but my petticoat caught on a nail and hung like a lace curtain, revealing my bloomers to all. Quick as I could, I straightened myself, but already the men were wide-eyed.

"Well, now," one of them said, "a sight that purty don't hurt my feelings at all, not one bit."

"Mine neither, no-how," said his friend, tipping his hat my way.

"Excuse me, gentlemen," I said, passing through the crowd with Josie, pretending everything was regular. "Our new duties await us."

The biggest surprise was that no one disputed me, not even my sister. She fell in step and went to work like she'd been doing this all along. Seeing as how she wanted to be an actress, I figured helping the postmistress was just a new role for her.

Ma insisted Whiskey Nose stay with us while his shoulder healed up, on account he lived alone in a stuffy hotel room with noise night and day. He had a bad cough that made us worry that his lungs got hurt, too. Tall Sing built a shelter for our patient outside in the garden. It was cool, with a nice breeze from the river.

I observed Tall Sing making a salve from wet sagebrush and deer grease, which he pressed onto the wound. He covered it with a clean rag and told Whiskey Nose to keep still so it wouldn't fall off.

Then Tall Sing turned to me. In his gentle voice he said, "Clemmy, this good med'cine keep infection away, swelling down. Use new cloth each day."

"All right."

Twice a day—after breakfast and just before sundown—Josie and I changed the bedding, which meant more work for Hap Wo's laundry, but Tall Sing said cleanliness was important. He also ordered our patient to bathe in the river.

Josie and I occupied ourselves elsewhere while Tall Sing helped him do this.

That first night under our care, Whiskey Nose thanked me for feeding him soup. There were tears in his eyes.

"Don't cry, now," I said. "You're gonna be all right." Then, feeling protective, I asked who had attacked him.

"Miss Clementine, I can't say."

"Can't?" I asked.

He responded by rolling on his pallet to face the river. There was an aroma of wood smoke from Tall Sing's campfire. He and several other Chinese were nearby, roasting trout on long sticks. Their pot of rice was in the coals.

I watched them for a while, hoping Whiskey Nose would continue our conversation. But when he didn't answer, I decided to let him rest. Seems he knew who had stabbed him and why, but that he wasn't about to say.

* * *

Pa showed up three nights later, after our customers had left. Ma brought him a bowl of her good vegetable soup, then sat beside him, looking into his rough face. If ever a man needed a shave and the dust rinsed from his hair, it was my father.

He took her hand and held it to his cheek, like to cool a burning inside him.

"Ruby June . . . oh, Ruby June," was all he said.

21

Fourth of July

Starting at midnight, the boom of gunpowder rang clear up into our canyon and, I reckoned, far across the valley. All through the night, explosions went off, to let anyone who dared sleep know that the Fourth of July was here. My first chore that morning was to cut pats of butter for the pancakes, then mix eggs, flour, and milk for the batter. By the time Ma, Josie, and I had eaten breakfast, a straggle of customers began appearing on the path on their way from town.

"All the little boys are running wild," said Jesse Blue in our doorway, removing his hat when he saw me. "A whole gang of 'em were on Main Street with Chinese crackers, long strings of 'em, scarin' the liver out of every cat 'n dog. Morning, Mrs. Kidd." He took his usual seat next to Shorty.

Across the table from them was Whiskey Nose, already on his third cup of coffee and chattering like a jay. Despite his wounded shoulder, he managed to shrug and gesture while trying to explain his point of view. He and Pa were engaged in another one of their peppery discussions.

Their subject? Finding a husband for me . . . again!

Since coming home from his three-day ride with the vigilantes, Pa had been more pensive than I had ever recollected. Something was weighing on his mind, that was certain. But for the moment, he seemed to be enjoying his debate with Whiskey Nose like it was just a regular day. At least this morning they were riled up on coffee instead of drink.

Still, it made me feel uppity to hear my name mentioned while I was standing right there at the stove.

"Papa," I said, "talk about something else . . . please!" As I poured batter onto our skillet, the cakes sizzled with a rich buttery aroma. I flipped them to brown on their other side, then set the cooked ones on the stove's warming rack. Poured more, flipped, waited, then stacked. Nine men at the table meant near sixty pancakes.

"Clementine's husband has got to be from a respectable family," said Pa, ignoring my plea. "An up-and-comer. Someone who knows the difference between a carriage and a mule wagon."

"You mean an older fella?" asked Jesse Blue, who had joined the conversation. He smiled up at me as I set a platter of crisp bacon on the table, the same hopeful look he'd given me outside the saloon. His raised eyebrow said that maybe Pa would put the two of *us* together, seeing as how he was an Old Forty-niner himself and could take care of me. To avoid Jesse Blue's friendly hand, I stepped out of his reach to where Pa was seated.

"Papa," I whispered in his ear, so no one else could hear, "those firecrackers coming from town mean it's Independence Day. Let's talk about George Washington."

Suddenly my father grew thoughtful. He set his fork down. "Now there's a man I admire," he said.

"*Who?*" asked everyone at the table at the same instant.

Still lost in thought, my father said, "Such dignity. Such . . . leadership."

At that, Jesse Blue and Whiskey Nose straightened their shoulders like the perfect gentlemen they wished themselves to be. Shorty took a careful sip of his coffee, not loud like regular. The other half-dozen miners regarded me with a wistful tenderness.

Only then did I figure that each man thought the name I had whispered to Pa was his own—my prospective husband! Even Ma and Josie looked at me with astonishment.

I meant to explain right away, truly I did. But their wonder filled me with an odd joy. If I had wanted to be a bride that very day, I could have been. The thought made me feel brave.

"Time for me to skedaddle!" I announced. I untied my apron to hang by the pantry, then put on my bonnet. "A stage is due this morning, gentlemen. There'll be mail, of course." I kissed Ma's cheek and was pleased to see Josie also hanging up her apron. The hat she plopped on her head was an old floppy thing she found in the river with a bullet hole through its brim.

Ma was the only one to wave good-bye as my sister and I went out the door. Pa and our customers had already resumed their discussion, Whiskey Nose the most lively of them all. He didn't seem at all disappointed that I was taking over his job and pay. I reckoned the other miners would be heading upriver to their claims—such as they were—soon as breakfast was over.

22
Anvil Firing

While patriotic thunder rattled the little window in the library, Josie and I organized all the reading material we'd dug out of the mail sacks. Among newspapers from New York and Philadelphia were back issues of *Harper's Weekly*, several dime novels, and a bundle of Peter Parley's children's books. Then in the post office my sister and I took turns reading aloud the names on the front of parcels and envelopes. This was so we could file them in the honeycomb shelf against the back wall, from A to Z. Now when folks came in for mail, it would be easier to help them.

The method Whiskey Nose had used was peculiar, wherein he stacked letters on the floor by shape, size and color. I once saw a shopkeeper kick the wall in frustration after waiting half an hour. "Good heavens, man," he had said. "Get a move on! This ain't a ladies' parlor."

By the time Josie and I finished, the morning had passed. Our fingers were black from ink and we were hungry. When Tall Sing appeared in the doorway with a small basket, only then did I remember we had forgotten to pack a lunch.

"Clemmy, you and Josie need eat," he said, putting it on the counter. "You like these."

I pulled back the white cloth to peek inside: thin cucumbers that we could eat like carrots and bright red strawberries. "Tall Sing, you're mighty good to us." I wanted to hug him like I would my pa, but knew if folks saw me do such a thing they would say it was improper.

Josie and I washed our hands in the half-full rain barrel and ate on the front steps. It was difficult to hear each other talk above the noise of firecrackers, but she asked if she could wander through town before the parade started, like all the other kids were doing.

I hesitated. My sister could land in trouble without even trying.

"May I, Clementine?" she asked again. "I ain't seen Penelope all week."

I glanced around at all the passersby. "All right," I said. "Let's meet at two o'clock, in front of City Market. Parade starts about then."

Her dimple showed in her smile. As she got ready to go, she said, "I like helping you, Clementine."

"Me too, Josie. I like your help."

She tucked her braids up under her hat. "So the Lester boys don't pull 'em," she explained. "Say, are you gonna marry Shorty? He sure do pretty-up his manners on account of you. Told me the other day you inspire him to write poetry."

Before I could answer, my sister was out the door with a skip, like a colt leaving a barn. I watched her go up Main Street until I could no longer see her hat among the crowd.

Then I tied on my bonnet, hung a closed sign in the post office window, and latched the door.

I hoped to find a current newspaper, to read if there was a report on the Wells Fargo bandits or on who stabbed Whiskey Nose. But when I got to the printing office, the editor had hung a Closed sign in his window as well.

Two blacksmiths were having a footrace down Main Street to the schoolyard, but they weren't running. They were doing a slow shuffle through the dirt, since each carried in his arms a heavy iron anvil from their livery stable. Their muscles bulged under rolled-up sleeves, and sweat stained the backs of their shirts. A crowd of men and boys ran ahead in the hot sun to cheer them on and I followed, recollecting from last year what would happen next.

When they reached the meadow, one of the smithies set his anvil out in the open. Dog Face Sam was waiting there with a sack of black powder, which he poured onto the anvil's flat surface. Next he laid out a long, white fuse that dropped to the grass. The second smithy brought over his anvil and set it upside down on the first one, so the two flat sides were together.

A sandwich is what came to mind, a dynamite sandwich.

Before you could count to ten, Dog Face Sam had struck a match against a stone, lit the fuse, and was yelling, "Run for your lives!"

I was on the schoolhouse step watching the spectacle of folks running into the woods as fast as they could, men holding on to their hats and ladies shrieking, children scattering every which way.

A boom shook the ground like cannon fire. Black smoke rose up with the explosive clank of iron upon iron. No one got killed that I could tell, but a small boy knocked himself out from running into a tree.

"That's anvil firing for you." A man's voice came from an open window of the schoolroom.

I was startled to see Boone Reno leaning out over the sill with a paintbrush. "Howdy, Clementine." His cheeks were sunburned, his brown hair curling out from under his hat.

"What're you doing in there, Boone?"

"Workin'."

"But it's a holiday. Stores are closing for the parade."

"Had a few touch-ups to finish," he said. "The dance is here tonight, you know."

"I figured as much."

"Would you come with me, Clementine? Me and my pa are gonna sit with your family at the picnic beforehand."

My eyes must've showed surprise on account he quick said, "Your pa invited us."

Boone disappeared for a moment, then came out the door with a bucket of whitewash. He was a head taller than I was and broad in the shoulders, a pleasingness I had not noticed before. We stood on the schoolhouse step looking out over the meadow.

Finally I said, "I reckon I'd like to dance with you, Boone."

23
Trouble in Bin Suey Alley

Three lawyers in their black coats and string ties stood by the podium, waiting their turns to give patriotic speeches. Judge Reno was near finished reading the Declaration of Independence to the crowd of picnickers. He was the handsomest man in Nugget, tall with a smooth face and his hair parted down the middle. He did not have the hardened, tired look I was used to seeing at our breakfast table.

Judge Reno didn't look like a vigilante.

On account of the heat, he had taken off his jacket and was in shirtsleeves with suspenders. The gold chain of his watch dangled from his pocket. By his relaxed manner I reckoned he slept in a feather bed and had never toiled outdoors in his life. I could see where Boone got his sturdy good looks.

The judge paused in his remarks, gazing out at all of us families sitting on blankets with our suppers, sharing pies and cakes with the bachelor miners. But then of all things, his eyes stopped on me! He gave a slow smile like we were well acquainted, but I swear we had only met that afternoon when Ma was passing around plates of chicken.

Pa leaned toward me. "Judgelikesyou, Clem'tine." His words were slurred.

The happiness I'd felt earlier dimmed, like a cloud moving over the sun. Folks were turning to see who was the object of Judge Reno's attention. I did not like how they regarded me, not one bit.

And I did not like that my father's breath stunk of whiskey.

By the time the dance started, Pa couldn't stand up straight. Ma tried to coax him home, but he shook off her hand.

"I'm goin't Shorty's," he said in such a loud voice both Ma and I turned around, hoping no one was watching. We whispered to him, but he only argued back.

The sunset was turning dark and a breeze was stirring high in the trees. Tall Sing came over with his lantern. "Home, Missus Kidd?" he asked my mother.

"Thank you, Tall Sing. It's been a long day. Clementine, do you see your sister?" Ma set her basket on the ground, then stood on her toes to look.

Suddenly we realized that in the commotion of my father being drunk in public, us being embarrassed about it, and swarms of people leaving the picnic, we'd lost sight of Josie.

"D'you suppose she went back to the cabin," I asked, "like she's done before?"

Ma picked up her basket. "Well, just in case she did, Tall Sing and I will head up there. Just promise me, darlin', that you'll let Boone or one of our friends escort you home."

When I turned the corner at Third Street, Boone was coming down the front porch of his house. He wore a clean blue shirt and his hair was slicked back. A sign nailed to the railing said LEROY H. RENO, JUDGE.

"Why, Clementine, what're you doing here? I was going to meet you—"

"I'm trying to find Josie," I cried.

He shut the gate to his picket fence. "Don't worry," he said. "We'll find her. Any idea where she's gone off to?"

I thought of Penelope and the dance hall. "This way," I said, heading toward Main Street. The stores were closed, but there were so many cafés and bars serving customers, the sidewalks were awash in yellow light from their windows. We looked in every one.

At Shorty's we saw Pa at a poker table dealing cards, a pile of blue and red chips in front of him. I suspected he would lose more than he might win, but my worry right then was for my sister.

When we came upon Whiskey Nose riding a donkey into Lucky Jim's—right through the double doors, calm as you please—I followed him. I knew I shouldn't, but I had to find Josie. He might have seen her.

This time when men's eyes turned my way, Boone came to my side and took my arm. Not like he was presuming anything of me, but protective-like. The starers turned away.

Meantime, there was Whiskey Nose on the back of his donkey and no one paying any mind to him at all.

"I'll have a triple shot," he told the bartender, "and a treat for my friend here." He patted the neck of his animal with the stump of his arm, then gestured to a large glass jug full of pickled eggs.

Without a wink or worry, the proprietor poured from a bottle into a tin cup, which he slid across the bar to Whiskey Nose. Then he rolled up his sleeve and reached into the jar, pulling out a shiny wet egg, the kind that have already been peeled.

At this the donkey smiled—honest, that is what it did—such that its big yellow teeth showed and its tongue curled out. The bartender offered the egg and quick as one-two, it was slurped up and gone. Satisfied with this transaction, Whiskey Nose now tipped his drink back in one gulp and smacked his lips.

"Whooee," he said, slamming his cup onto the counter, "now that's what I call a spang-dangled whistle-kisser, happynewyear, everyone! Come on, Puddin'head, time to get goin'." He dropped a coin into the empty cup, then turned his donkey with his reins and rode toward the back of the saloon. Two men playing billiards interrupted their game to open the door for him, giving a friendly nod as he passed by.

"Comes every night," Boone said to me. "Except for when he got stabbed and was up to your place gettin' took care of."

I had missed the moment to ask Whiskey Nose about my sister, and, thinking it prudent not to call out her name, I elbowed my way to the sidewalk out front, mindful to step around the vomitous puddles.

As Boone and I continued down the block, I glanced up all the dimly lit side streets. When we came to Bin Suey Alley, I saw a girl enter one of the cabins. In the glow of the red paper lantern hanging on a post, she looked like Penelope. And there was a shadow of someone else with her.

"Hello?" I called, but Boone grabbed my arm.

"You don't wanna go down there," he said.

"But what if that's Penelope? She might know where Josie is." I pulled away from him and started walking.

"Clementine." Boone's voice was so gentle I stopped, but did not turn to look at him. A feeling of dread had made my mouth go dry.

"What's the matter?" I whispered.

"Clementine, that's an opium den."

24
A Young Addict

"Opium?" I could scarce say the word.

Boone gazed up the alley, nodding. "I myself have warned Josie about the danger. D'you reckon she'd go to such a place anyhow?"

"We have to look!"

He responded by touching my elbow and striding ahead. The other shacks and cottages had windows with lamplight turned low, their doors open for the cool night air. I could hear voices from inside speaking Chinese, and there were familiar cooking aromas, like those from Tall Sing's campfire—sesame oil and ginger.

When we came to the cabin where the girl had entered, Boone knocked on the door. I found a brick to stand on, to look in a window. Its torn curtain gave me a glimpse into a room lit with candles on the floor. From a bullet hole in the glass came a sickening sweet smell.

Inside was a Chinese man reclining on a cushion, smoking a tiny pipe. He was bald except for a patch of hair at the back of his head, which was braided and draped over his arm. In the dim light it was hard to see faces, but finally I recognized Penelope, also lying on a cushion.

And next to her, there was no mistaking my sister, with her pigtails and slouch hat. The man was offering his pipe to her.

"Josie!" I screamed at the window. "Don't!"

That did it for Boone. He kicked in the door. In two steps he reached my sister, hauled her over his shoulder like a sack of beans, then brought her out into the fresh air. By the time he set her on the ground, she was still too surprised to speak. She gave us a scared look, like we were bears come out of the woods.

"Josie Kidd!" I was mad and worried all at once. "What are you doing here?"

"Penny wanted me to meet her friends. They're real nice, Clementine."

"*Nice?* Josie, this is a viper's nest!" I looked at Boone. "We can't leave Penelope. She's only fourteen."

At that, Boone disappeared into the smoky room. Quick as a heartbeat, he was outside with Penelope in his arms, her head hung back, eyes closed. Even in the lamplight I saw that her face was ashen.

"What's wrong with her?" Josie asked.

"She'll be like this for hours," said Boone. "Then she'll wake up sick in her head and wanting to come back here to smoke some more, thinkin' she'll feel better again, only she'll get worse day by day. Josie, where's this girl live? We're taking her home."

* * *

Josie led us to the dance hall across the street from Shorty's, where I'd seen the two of them together before.

"Upstairs." She pointed when we came through the swinging doors. The room was smoky and loud with fiddle music. I heard clinks of coins at the poker tables even above the noise of men cheering one another in a game of darts. Ma would be appalled to know I'd now entered two saloons in one night.

Eyes followed us up the rickety steps, but no one stopped Boone to ask why he was carrying one of their dancing girls.

We followed Josie down a dark hall until she opened a door at the end. The room was narrow with two cots and a washstand. On the stand was a pitcher of water, a bowl and a bar of soap. A window let in light from the street, where folks were still shooting off Chinese crackers. I opened it for a breeze as Boone settled Penelope onto one of the beds.

Then I untied the rope of her shoes and took them off. Found a cloth to wash her face. She was in a dreamy state, talking but making no sense. Her eyes rolled when she tried to look at me. Right then I determined to ask Tall Sing to teach me how to cure this sickness.

"Josie," I said, "where's Penelope's aunt, the one she lives with?"

"Dancin'. I seen her downstairs."

Boone turned for the door. "I'll go fetch 'er."

After making sure Penelope wouldn't be alone, we headed up the canyon. Boone escorted us with his lantern to make sure we didn't wander from the trail.

"Ain't never goin' to those places again, I promise," Josie said, taking off her hat to hold over her heart. "Clementine, please don't tell Ma. It grieves me awful when she's mad at me."

I gave her braid a tug.

We crossed the footbridge with Boone in front, holding his lamp high so we could watch our steps, careful as ever. The river was white where it splashed among the rocks. I could feel its mist on my face.

Up ahead was the welcoming light of our cabin, Tall Sing out front with the rifle. When we saw Ma standing in the doorway, Josie ran into her skirt and hugged her fierce.

Ma's face was stern, but she nodded to Boone. "Thank you for bringing my girls home. Won't you stay for pie? I'll put on a pot of coffee."

"Sounds too good to pass up, Mrs. Kidd. Thanks muchly."

Ma went over to the oven and opened the iron door. Grasping the sides of her apron, she reached in and pulled out a large, golden-crusted pie: apple with butter, cinnamon, and brown sugar, my favorite. Oh, did it smell delicious.

At the table, moths fluttered around the glass dome of our oil lamp as we ate dessert for the second time that night. There were five of us on account Ma insisted Tall Sing join us. He watched the door.

It was peaceful with Pa not there.

25

Hidden from the Trail

As summer moved further into July, the days grew hot. I was grateful for afternoon thunderstorms that cooled the air. Clouds would tower behind the mountain and soon darken the sky. Thunder lasted only a few minutes, but the rain that came with it was enough to spatter the dirt and give rise to the sweet scent of sagebrush.

It was just such a hot day that I closed the library and post office before noon. I had cleaned the windows, swept the floors, and sorted all the mail and books. The next stage wasn't due until the morrow, so I put a sign on the door saying so. When I returned to our cabin, Josie was slicing potatoes for stew, while Ma braised meat in the skillet.

My sister's list of chores was long on account Ma was trying to keep her busy, to keep her out of trouble. We ate melon and cucumbers for lunch, then I went to the garden to help Tall Sing. His face was shaded under his hat, and he greeted me with one for myself. When I put it on, its brim cooled me like a parasol.

"Friend give to me," he said, "to pay for med'cine. Now come, Clemmy, I show you something." He led me to a trail through the woods. As we hiked under the blazing sun, I looked up at the clouds in hope that it would rain. The hillsides were carpeted with brown pine needles baking in the heat, giving off a sleepy aroma. I could also smell wild onions and mint as I followed him up a streambed into the brush.

"Watch out," said Tall Sing. He pointed to a man-sized hole, partially covered with a crisscross of boards that may or may not have kept someone from falling in. These abandoned shafts scared me. I wished miners would fill them in when they couldn't find a vein of ore. Some of these pits went down so far you couldn't see the bottom.

We soon came to a hedge of chokecherries, the branches spotted red from its ripe fruit. To my surprise, hidden inside this hedge was a tiny cabin. If not for Tall Sing, I never would have seen it from the path.

He unhooked the door, then ducked to enter. Inside was a bed on stilts with a table and chair beneath it. On the other wall by a window was a shelf of bottles and jars, and a carving knife. The iron stove in the corner was the size of a herring box, that is to say, small, like a short stack of books. Its pipe poked up through the roof. The ceiling was so low Tall Sing had to stoop to move around. I could feel the top of my head brush against the wood. Hanging upside down from the beams were bouquets of herbs and flowers, in various stages of drying.

I looked around the small room. When I saw the doll—a Chinese girl dressed in a silk tunic—some early memories came to me of Tall Sing talking about daughters of his own back in Canton. He hadn't mentioned them in a long time.

"What is this place?" I asked him.

His wrinkled face creased into a smile. "Solitude. Nobody know but you, Clemmy."

Sunlight slanted through the window and open door. A breeze rustled the pages of a book on his bed. From outside I could hear the trickle of a creek and birds singing, a meadowlark and killdeer. Marmots were whistling to one another from their rocky playground. After a long moment I realized what was missing: the pounding noise of stamp mills that I had grown so accustomed to.

It *was* quiet.

I stepped out into the shade of a blue spruce, the wind whooshing through its branches, then climbed onto a boulder that protected one side of the cabin. From this perch I could see the hills for miles around. On a faraway ridge, a road curved down toward the valley and, I reckoned, Boise City. A team of mules was pulling a wagon up the steep grade, plumes of dust in its wake.

In another direction my eyes followed a gulley that led down to the river. There, plain as you please, were Ma and Josie at a sandbar on Bear Creek washing dishes! Just steps away from our own cabin.

Tall Sing laughed at my astonishment.

This gave me pause. I never thought Tall Sing might want to be alone, never in all the years he'd lived with us. But it figured he would not let himself be far from us. If Josie, Ma, or I needed him, he could hear our voices, this canyon was that quiet. And Tall Sing was that devoted to our family.

I looked up at him from under the speckled straw of my hat. My question came out as a whisper. "Why do you stay with us? Don't you miss your little girls?"

"Ah." He put a coil of rope into his basket, then walked uphill to a clearing.

I followed. Wondering.

Tall Sing tied one end of the rope to a tree, then spread it in the grass, making a loopy knot. In the center of this loop he put a stub of bright orange carrot and some cabbage leaves. Then he crept backwards across the clearing, feeding the length of rope through his fingers until he was hidden behind a bush.

Through the branches I could see the blue sleeve of his smock and that he was patting the dirt for me to join him there. I crawled under a bough.

He put his fingers to his lips, signaling me to stay quiet.

We waited. The stillness hummed with cicadas. In the heat, my throat ached with thirst, and once again I looked to the sky. No clouds yet. This was not the moment to ask Tall Sing about the opium sickness. Or to ask about his family.

Suddenly his arm jerked, then there was rustling in the grass. A large white-tailed jackrabbit was struggling to free its front paw from the rope. It was panicked, hopping wildly on its huge hind feet, like a bucking mule. Oh, it was a handsome creature.

Tall Sing crept toward it. He grabbed the frightened animal by the scruff of its neck, then cradled it in his arms.

Speaking to it in Chinese, he stroked its long ears that lay over its back.

"Come out now, Clemmy. See how easy to catch?"

"But Ma's already got dinner going," I said.

"This not for kettle."

"But why—"

"To show you how." Tall Sing then unlooped the rope, freeing the rabbit. With one great bound it disappeared into the trees.

Marbled clouds were boiling up behind the mountain when Tall Sing latched the door of his cabin and we headed back down the gulley. It was still hot, but thunder rumbled in the distance, and I could smell rain.

I puzzled over Tall Sing's quiet cabin and why he had shown me how to catch a rabbit. Like Ma, was he worried about what Pa might do to our family?

Now everyone had a secret.

26
Another Hanging

It was still hot the next day when Dog Face Sam came into the post office.

It was hard for my eyes not to drift to his disfigured cheek. Scar tissue covered the bullet hole and the end of his nose, creating a hideous red lump. The line where his stitches had been looked like railroad tracks. I reckoned I could have sewn him up better than his surgeon had, on account that we ladies are dainty with needle and thread.

The poor man smelled like rotten onions.

When he told me his real name was Samuel Peter LaBrea, I turned to the wall and looked in the L slot.

"Here you go, sir." I handed him a letter postmarked from Los Angeles, dated January 20, 1865. It had taken just six months to be delivered.

"Thank you, Miss Clementine, but you best close up shop and get home now. The thief that stabbed Whiskey Nose confessed last night. Gettin' strung up at noon."

"What? Do you mean . . . hanged?"

"Yep, and a pretty gal such as yourself ought not to see such a sight."

"But, there hasn't been a trial," I said. "Whiskey Nose didn't die, so why—"

"A considerable amount of gold was took from his person," said Dog Face Sam, "and already spent. Last night at Lucky Jim's, Whiskey Nose and the robber had a long conversation. He begged us not to make an arrest, but the law's the law. And with the sheriff outta town, someone's got to uphold it."

In my mind I tried to picture Whiskey Nose on his donkey, ordering rum and a pickled egg, then talking to the thief. "Doesn't seem like proper justice to me," I said.

"Well, Miss Clementine, you leave that to us. Just get yourself home in case there's trouble. You know how worked up folks can get over these sorts of things."

After Dog Face Sam left, I closed the post office, pondering what he meant by "us." Was Pa involved? And where was Judge Reno in all this?

I stepped out onto the sidewalk. Dust rose from the street like a regular day, but more so at the edge of town where men were gathering near a large oak tree. A few Chinese were quick-stepping away from there, their shoulder baskets swinging.

I looked at the sun overhead. If someone was going to be hanged at noon—murdered, to my mind—well, I wanted to be far away.

As I hurried up Main Street, an anguished cry made me

turn around. A female was screaming, "No! No!" When I realized the voice was my sister's, I grabbed the hem of my skirt and ran toward the tree.

Josie burst from the crowd, sprinting in my direction like a panicked rabbit. She was waving her hat, bawling like I'd never seen before.

"Clementine!" she cried. "Hurry!"

I caught her in my arms and held her tight as I could. By then Ma had come out of the bakery and was running, too.

"What's wrong?" we asked her.

Josie pointed to the men, trying to catch her breath, pulling our hands to go back with her. "Come quick," she said. "They're gonna hang Penelope!"

27
The Noose

I had never seen my mother in such a fury. She marched to the tree, into that crowd, such that the men scattered like birds.

"What in the name of common sense are you fools doing? Can't you see this girl is just a child?" She gestured toward Penelope, who was sitting on the back of a horse, arms tied behind her and a thick rope around her neck. Jesse Blue was holding the horse's reins.

Without waiting for an answer, Ma walked up to him and slapped his cheek so hard his head turned.

"Ma'am," he said.

"Don't ma'am me, Jesse Blue. You get her down from there. *Now.*"

When he hesitated, Ma slapped his other cheek. My eyes went up to the rope where it was tied to a thick branch. I felt nervous on account he could have let the horse bolt out from under Penelope right then, hanging her on the spot. But instead of that occurring, Ma stepped into one of the stirrups, boosting herself high enough to lift the noose from Penny's head. Then she eased the girl out of the saddle and both of them slipped to the ground.

I rushed forward to help catch Penny and untie her hands.

"Thank you . . . oh, thank you." She rubbed her wrists, then her neck. Upon seeing Josie, she broke down crying, hugging both of us at the same time.

Whiskey Nose burst from the crowd where someone had been holding him back. He was rubbing the stump of his arm like it was sore, and he was coughing bad. "You ring-tailed rats!" he yelled. "I told you I ain't gonna press charges!"

Now Ma faced the vigilantes. "How dare you call your-selves men? You ought to be ashamed of yourselves. Until Judge Reno can hear all the facts, this child will be staying under my roof."

One of the gamblers I'd seen at Shorty's stepped forward with his hand on his holster. "And just who d'you think *you* are, madam? This ain't none of your beeswax."

I could feel Penelope tremble in my embrace. For a moment I worried the crowd might turn on us ladies. Anger burned in me, thinking how my father was still up at our cabin sleeping off his rough night.

I looked for Tall Sing, relieved *he* wasn't there. It was the sort of situation where he could get lynched himself, if he tried to help us.

Ma wasn't afraid, though. She looked the gambler square

in the eye. "Put your gun away, mister," she said. "This town doesn't need another coward."

All the way up Gold Digger's Canyon my knees felt weak, yet I had not been the one with a noose around my neck. I kept turning around, glad no one was following us.

While we were crossing the footbridge, Josie was in front of me like regular. Don't know how it happened, but all of a sudden she slipped and fell into the rapids. Without a thought, I grabbed the back of her dress just as the current pushed her head under water. Out the corner of my eye, I noticed Ma on the far shore, her mouth open with a scream.

Lowering myself to my stomach, I held on to Josie, trying to clutch her flailing hands. By a miracle her fingers were able to find mine and I eased her closer to me. The instant her head popped up, she gasped for air, choking and retching.

"Hang on, Josie!" I cried above the roaring water.

Just when I thought my strength would give out, strong arms were pulling my sister from the river. Tall Sing was next to me, stretched out along the footbridge, his long pigtail floating on the surface like a ribbon.

"One . . . two . . ." he yelled, ". . . up, Josie!" And there she was, soaked like a dishrag and shivering. She seemed too stunned to cry even as she watched her favorite hat drift around the bend and disappear.

I lay there for a moment, waiting for my heart to slow down. Tall Sing carried Josie to the other side, his bare feet taking measured steps along the wet log. His sleeves were dripping.

When he set her on the bank, she ran to our mother.

"Oh, Ma," she said, "today me and Penny near landed ourselves in Heaven, the both of us. D'you reckon God ain't ready for us yet?"

All color had gone out of Ma's face. "I reckon not, Josie."

28
Ma's Cookbook

Autumn soon was upon us. Day by day, the sun moved lower in the sky, and at night the thermometer dropped below freezing. Frost touched the hills, turning the aspen to yellow, and brush along the river a bright red. Wind stirred the air with falling leaves. The cooler weather put a skip in my heart, made me feel hopeful somehow. Even Josie was glad to be back in school to see her friends and teacher.

Folks in Nugget were also feeling perked up on account of several curious events:

One, that we had survived the first summer in years without a forest fire. As Providence would have it, each lightning strike had been snuffed out by rain before it could torch the timber. And in town, not one store or stable had burned down. It was the only mining camp I had lived in that didn't go up in flames.

The second event was that Penelope promised to repay the money she stole from Whiskey Nose. Said she hadn't been in her right mind, that she was sorry as could be about stabbing him.

"All's well that ends well," he said, waving away all of us who worried about his deep cough, new since the knife wound.

Judge Reno stamped a paper signed by the both of them, then put it in his filing cabinet. This agreement took place in his living room, with the divan pushed aside so all of us could be witnesses. Ma had sewed Penny a blue gingham dress for the occasion, and I bought her a pair of shoes from my earnings as postmistress, three dollars at the mercantile. Josie gave her a bow for her hair. All was cordial, and the judge allowed her to move back to the saloon with her aunt.

A third event that got folks talking was Boone Reno asked Pa if he could court me. My father's immediate reply was, "Boy howdy, yes!" without either of them consulting me. For several days afterward, the men around our dinner table were gloomy—especially Shorty—most of them wishing they'd beat Boone to the asking. I didn't want to give any of them false hopes by arguing with Pa.

Josie was beside herself. "Clementine, this is the gladdest news I ever did hear." She and I were in Tall Sing's garden, digging up the last of his radishes and turnips.

"Why on earth do you say that?" I asked.

"Now you'll be getting' married, and Boone will be my brother."

I reached to Josie's cheek to brush aside a strand of hair that had turned white in the sun since losing her hat. Her nose was freckled and she had a certain sparkle in her eye that hinted of mischief. She was the sturdiest little sister anyone could have.

"Josie," I said, "Boone is a dear fellow. He makes an honest living and he's kind to our family. I feel good when I'm with him, but—"

"But what?" A shadow crossed Josie's face.

I shrugged, trying to find the words. "Josie, it's just that I'm not looking for a husband. At least not now."

"But he likes you, Clementine. Told me himself. He's even building a little cabin up Cougar Creek so he don't have to live with his pa no more. Ain't far from here." Josie pointed up the canyon toward the North Fork. Her hands and fingernails were black with soil from the garden. I smiled. Not only was my sister a hard worker, she was hopeful about so many things.

"We'll see," I told her. "Courtship is for folks to get acquainted. Maybe Boone will change his mind when he finds out I can be grouchy and fussy."

Josie laughed out loud and grabbed me in a hug.

I said, "Who knows what'll happen, Josie? Maybe I love Boone already and don't even know it. Now get one of those pumpkins and I'll race you to the cabin."

Ma's cookbook was on a pantry shelf. She practically knew it by heart, but me, I always forgot how much salt and sugar for a pumpkin pie. I was flipping through its pages when a sheet of newsprint fell out, folded so only the blank side showed.

I glanced at the table where Ma was helping Josie pour coffee beans into our grinder. I leaned into the shelf so they couldn't see my hands and quiet-like opened up the *Gazette*.

It was months old, dated Thursday, July 5. I wondered

how I could have missed seeing this edition in town. There hadn't even been one for the library.

STAGE ROBBERS GONE FOR GOOD
15-YEAR-OLD LAD WAS PART OF GANG

Real quick, I read the story: Vigilantes had caught up to the outlaws in their hideout up Wolf Paw Canyon. "The uncooperative perpetrators were dispatched," the report said, "by a volley of Colt .44s, never again to see the light of day. Hallelujah. The quicker Idaho Territory gets rid of these sorts of vermin, the quicker we'll reach statehood and national respectability."

My eyes scanned the newspaper's three columns. No names were mentioned. Not the vigilantes', nor the bandits'.

Ma must have had suspicions, too.

29
Gifts

Week by week Josie gave me the few coins she earned by helping Ma. I waited until she was asleep at night before adding them to my hiding spot. Did not want her to be tempted to blurt out its location to Pa. For that reason, I didn't tell Ma either.

Meantime, Pa was trying real hard to be his good self.

One September afternoon, he hobbled up the path with three parcels in his arm. They were wrapped in brown paper, tied with string. He was smiling like the old days.

"Josie, honey," he said, sitting by the fire. "Come on over here. This is for you." He handed her a bumpy, oblong package.

Her eyes were wide as she ripped away the paper. "Thank you, Papa!" she said real quick, so as not to show her disappointment. It was a porcelain doll in a satin dress with tiny leather boots. Though Josie was still what most folks considered a little girl, she hadn't played with dolls for years. But she threw her arms around Pa's neck, thanking him over and over. "I'll take care of her forever, Papa."

Ma's gift was a swath of calico, yellow with white edging.

"So you can make yourself a new dress, Ruby June. You look so pretty in yellow."

Ma unfolded the cloth. There was only an arm's length, not enough for a dress, not even a blouse. Pa seemed all at once to realize this, but Ma was quick to comfort him. "No matter, Dallas. I need a new curtain for the window. It'll work fine, and yellow will be cheerful this winter. Thank you, dear."

My package was the smallest—a bundle of hair ribbons in rainbow colors. Pa hadn't noticed that I'd been swirling my braid on top of my head, like Ma. On account that Boone and I were courting, I wanted to be ladylike. "Thank you Papa," I said, hugging him.

Eleven miners crowded around our table that night, for Ma's good stew, Josie's biscuits, and my pumpkin pie. But in the middle of supper, Pa suddenly got up for his hat and kissed Ma good-bye. Her face showed the same surprise I felt. Josie was the one who protested.

"Please stay, Papa!" she cried. "We can play checkers again. I like my doll, I really do. Don't go."

Our customers kept their eyes on their plates, their conversations quiet.

"Honey, I got some business in town," Pa said. "Now mind your ma and I'll see you for breakfast. That's my good girl."

When Pa limped out the door, Josie crossed her arms. She did not finish her supper.

* * *

After the miners had finished their coffee and bid us good evening, we cleared the table. Ma put some of their coins in the dirt hole under our butter churn.

"But Papa will look there," Josie said. "Then he'll lose everything at poker."

"You're right, Josie. But at least this way he'll come home to us and we can give him a hot meal." Ma glanced over at me wiping the cups and putting them on the shelf. I knew she had another reason for letting Pa find money.

He hadn't pulled another knife on us, true, but sometimes in the middle of the night we heard him move the butter churn—real gentle so as not to spill Ma's hard work—then we'd hear the clink of coins as he scooped them from the dirt.

This way Pa no longer tore apart the cabin searching. And my mother's cache behind the chimney stayed safe.

These habits were not the best for any of us, but somehow it felt like we were still family. I believed the reason Pa hadn't asked *me* for some silver dollars was that he still had decency when it came to his daughters.

30

The Assayer

We woke the next morning to a storm brewing. It was our day to visit the assayer, so Josie and I hurried to dress. Instead of putting my hair up fancy, I made a quick braid with one of Pa's ribbons. Then I hid Ma's leather pouch under my shawl.

Wind was blowing leaves across the trail as we headed for town. We walked fast to keep warm. Mountain bluebirds were taking flight for their southward journey, and squirrels were running up trees and leaping from branches. In their tiny mouths they carried walnuts near as big as their heads.

Dark clouds were building in the sky. Overhead were Vs of geese, honking to one another in the wind. We also heard the bugling of elk. I wasn't surprised, then, when we came around a bend to see two huge males standing in the shallows of the river, their antlers clacking as they butted each other. We hurried past without even a whisper so as not to startle them. If those bulls got mad, they could charge and trample us.

In town, I opened the library and post office for just one

hour, then tacked a note on the door saying I would return on the morrow. A light snow was falling. By the time Josie and I got to the assayer's office, puddles on the street were crusted with ice. A lady was coming out his door, her shawl pulled over her head against the cold.

The assayer took Ma's pouch to his worktable, where there was a mortar with pestle and a tiny set of scales. Jars and bottles of chemicals were on shelves around the cluttered room. It was a laboratory of sorts, with a furnace to test the ore that miners brought to him, to check the content of gold or silver.

All seemed proper, but I was suspicious of this man. The nails on his right thumb and forefinger were long. Rumors were that he pinched the dust in such a way as to save some for himself, thereby putting less on the scale.

Another trick—and I had witnessed this myself back in California—was that a thieving assayer would oil his hair, then run his fingers over his scalp so that gold flakes under his nails would stick to his head. Upon getting home he would shampoo himself in a basin, then gather the color. It was another way for cheaters to take what wasn't theirs.

This is why I tried to keep my eye on this fellow, asking him this and that so he'd know I was paying attention, but truth be told I was distracted by the swirling snowflakes outside. If we didn't hurry, our trail home would be impossible to see.

Also I had noticed Tall Sing across the street. He was waiting in line with his Chinese friends to pay the Mongolian Tax—four dollars every month—for their privilege of living in Idaho Territory. They couldn't see the gang of boys in slouch hats and suspenders who were swaggering along the sidewalk toward them. When I recognized Josie's tormentors, the Lester brothers, I knew there would be trouble. The older boy, Jim, carried a stick. Without warning, he struck Tall Sing and two friends behind the knees, knocking them down.

I bolted out the door, no longer concerned about Ma's gold.

The Lesters were cursing and using crude hand gestures. "Go back to China, you stinking coolies!" they yelled. "Celestial devils!" Then, at the sight of my shawl flapping in the wind, the boys turned on *me*.

"Well, lookie who thinks she's the Queen of Sheba," said Jim Lester. He cleared his throat with a loud spit that landed on Tall Sing's trousers. Then he walked toward me until the toes of our shoes were touching. "What're y'gonna do about it, Queenie?" His breath was hot in my face.

"Leave . . . them . . . alone," I said. I brought my fist up to his chin, just touching his prickly whiskers. How I wanted to thrash him. I could have with one swing, I was that mad.

Now Josie was running across the street, but someone was with her.

A figure came up beside me so fast I didn't realize it was Boone until he shoved Jim Lester to the ground. Then he grabbed him by his shirt, Billy Lester too, and knocked their heads together. That sent the rest of the gang down an alley, cussing at us over their shoulders as they scattered in different directions.

Boone held on to the Lester boys. He said, "You cowards ever do this again, you'll have me to answer to." He let them go, then picked up the stick like he intended to use it. Those brothers ran pell-mell.

Tall Sing and his friends were on their feet, brushing themselves off. They seemed fine, but Boone still went over to them. "I'm sure sorry about this," he told them. "Those kids got no call to bother you." Then he came to me.

"Clem, you all right? I won't stand for anyone hurtin' you."

"I'm fine, Boone."

We headed back to the assayer. Don't know what came over me, but when Boone's arm brushed against mine I slipped my hand in his. He held it nice and easy, and didn't let go.

31
Three Shots

The four of us—Boone, Josie, Tall Sing, and I—walked home in snow up to our ankles. Wind blew cold flakes down my neck.

I had been so lathered up about those boys that I barely heard the assayer as he counted out thirty dollars in silver coin, equal to—what *he* calculated—the gold nuggets we'd given him. Plus he charged me $1.50 for his labor. There was no way to know if it was a fair exchange, but I tucked Ma's pouch in my waist and bid him good afternoon. From the sidewalk I saw him watching me through the window and consoled myself with one thought: Honest or not, someday that man would have to answer to God.

On account of the storm, our hike up Gold Digger's Canyon was slow. When we came around the bend and saw the same two elk standing in the river, I felt something was wrong. They were still head-to-head, but in water now up to their bellies. They were panting, their tongues swollen. Snow covered their backs like blankets.

"Well, I'll be," said Boone. He stepped to the bank to better see them. "Their antlers are locked together."

"They've been here for hours," Josie said, giving me a worried look. "What's gonna happen to them?"

Boone shook his head. "See how tired they are, Josie, and thirsty? Probably been trapped like this since yesterday. Won't be long before their legs give out and the river takes 'em."

"They'll drown?"

"Reckon so." Boone rubbed his arms for warmth. I could hear the hiss of snowflakes as they landed on his jacket.

I was distressed by the sight of these doomed elk. Such magnificent creatures. I watched their heaving sides, their breath making steam in the cold air. Their eyes were glazed as if they could no longer see. The fight had been taken out of them as they'd tried to untangle themselves.

Josie turned to me. "Clementine, we have to do somethin'."

We studied them for some moments. Finally I said, "I have an idea."

Pa's rifle was over the door. When Josie saw me take it down she cried, "It ain't right to shoot 'em. Please, Clementine, don't."

I rolled the cylinder to make sure it was loaded. "Just come with me," I said. "You too, Boone?"

"Yep." He put his hat back on and opened the door for us.

Ma was already pouring Tall Sing a cup of hot tea. She had made him stand by the fire so he could warm up. They watched us leave.

Outside, our footprints from earlier were already hidden by new snow. "We have to hurry," I said. It was late afternoon.

We reached the elk, Josie running ahead. They did not seem afraid by our presence, such was their exhaustion. Real quick, I pulled the ribbon from the end of my braid, tied it around the thin trunk of a lodgepole pine, and made a loop of it. Through this loop I slipped in the barrel of Pa's rifle, twirling it until the ribbon tightened it against the tree like a vise. Now it was steady enough to aim.

Josie sucked in her breath. In a whisper she again pleaded with me. "Don't hurt them, Clementine."

I cocked the lever, then squinted through the sight until the racks of antlers were in view, focusing on where the two of them were joined. I counted to three. Slow and careful I squeezed the trigger. The blast knocked me backward, but a point of antler broke off and flew into the river. I repositioned myself, cocked, and fired again. Then once more. As the third shot hit, the racks broke apart enough so the bulls could separate.

I was relieved to see no blood. Not even their fur had been grazed. Pa had taught me well.

For a moment the animals stood as if in shock. One moved his head. As he drew back, he lost his balance and fell into the water. The splash of his large body sent a wave onto the bank.

"He's drownin'!" Josie cried.

"Wait," I said. We watched as the bull drifted head-high in the current over to the far bank. He found his footing on the rocky bottom, climbed out, then loped into the trees, the jagged rack on his head knocking snow from the low branches.

"That fella will be just fine," said Boone.

Meantime, the other bull stared at us. As if understanding that we meant him no harm, he made his way onto shore, so close I could smell the musk of his wet fur.

I quick untied my ribbon from the tree, shouldered the gun, and returned to the trail with Josie and Boone. The wind stung my face with snow and tangled my skirt around my knees. The footbridge was so icy, we crawled across so as not to slip. By the time we saw the welcoming smoke of Ma's chimney, my fingers ached from the cold. The wind had unraveled my braid so that my hair fell loose.

Boone opened the door, letting Josie go first into our warm cabin. Then he turned to me, regarding my wild hair with a smile. To my surprise, he put his hands around my waist and whispered in my ear.

"I'd sure fancy havin' a moment alone with you, Clem."

If Ma noticed me blushing when she hung up my wet shawl, she didn't let on.

32
A Familiar Dress

Our supper table was crowded. Even Pa was there. He shook hands with Boone.

"Sit here by me," Pa said to him. "Tell me how you're doin', son. It's good to see you." I felt heartened that my father was sober.

Despite it being winter, some prospectors were still upriver breaking ice on the shallow creeks to keep at their claims. They worked through all types of storms, but last January three men we knew got so sick with pneumonia, they were dead by February. It was the only reason I was glad Pa spent his days in a saloon. His name Dry Boots Kidd didn't bother me anymore.

There must've been ten conversations going on at once while Ma and I passed around the platter of roast venison, the bowls of beans, and plates of bread with butter. I glanced at Boone every chance I got, and he kept a pleasing eye on me.

At last, when all the food was served, I seated myself next

to him on the bench. With so many people close together, no one could see that Boone and I were holding hands under the table. However, when Ma noticed I was eating with my left hand—I am right-handed—she bit her lip to hide a smile.

Boone whispered at my ear. "I'm gonna call you Miss True Shot, and make sure I stay on your good side."

"Now, Boone," I whispered back, as Josie watched us, trying to eavesdrop, "if you make me mad, I'll let you know in plenty of time so you can get out of the way."

"Right kind of you, Clem. I'll remember that."

When it was time for dessert, I took Ma's steaming peach cobbler from the oven. Then I went around the table scooping some onto everyone's plate. That's when the miners began teasing Whiskey Nose.

". . . you rich yet?"

Whiskey Nose rubbed his arm where his hand used to be. His cough seemed worse. "Drat this cold weather," he said, wheezing. "I'll never get used to it."

I felt soft toward Whiskey Nose as he tried to change the subject. But his friends wouldn't let him.

"How much has she paid you?" one of them asked.

"If it keeps snowin' like this, me and Puddin'head will have to move down to Boise City—"

"Ah, cut the salami," said a man across the table from him so loud the room fell silent. "When're you gonna admit that dancin' gal ain't paid you a wooden nickel and probably won't never?"

Whiskey Nose turned red, honest he did. "Shaddup," he said. "This ain't none of your where-with-all."

Just then I recollected something unpleasant from the morning. So much had happened since then, I had forgotten until now.

It was on our walk from the post office. The lady we'd seen leaving the assayer was hidden under a cloak, yet her dress had seemed familiar. It was blue gingham like Ma had sewn for Penelope. When this lady went around the corner, wind blew her hood such that I saw her face. It *was* Penny, and she was headed up Bin Suey Alley.

Boone was right about the opium sickness.

A foot of snow had fallen by the time our customers buttoned up their coats for their tramp down the canyon into town. It would be like this after every storm, their needing to break a trail through the drifts.

I wrapped up in my shawl and stepped outside with Boone. Josie's face was at the window until I saw Ma's hand on her shoulder, drawing her away. Then Ma closed the curtain, the one she had finished sewing that morning.

"Stay warm," I instructed Boone. "And stay on the trail with the fellows so none of you get lost. It's still snowing."

"Darlin' Clementine, I don't know how I've managed all these years without your supervision."

We looked at each other like we wanted to keep the conversation going, but it was miserable cold. Frost from our breathing hung between us.

"Well, I'll be going now," Boone said. "See you tomorrow, I hope." He shook the snow off his hat, then picked up his lantern.

"Night, Boone."

"Night, Miss True Shot."

33
Full Moon

After watching Boone's lantern fade on the trail, I hurried inside to warm up. Josie and I swept the cabin and put clean dishes in the cupboard, then set another log on the fire. Ma didn't say so, and neither did we, but there was calm in our family that night.

Pa had been a perfect gentleman all evening.

I buried myself under our quilt. In my mind, I could still see Boone and how his blue eyes regarded me. Real gentle.

Somewhere in the wee hours I woke to a hand shaking my shoulder. I bolted up. But it was just Ma, whispering, "Come on, girls. It's a full moon."

Josie and I dressed in our wool leggings, boots, and hooded cloaks, then followed Ma out into the cold. The thermometer by the door read ten degrees below zero. We nudged each other, excited Ma had remembered our tradition: First full moon with snow, we would bathe in the hot spring.

The wind had stopped. Our breath looked like puffs of

smoke as we stood there a moment, taking in the beauty. The forested hills glowed from moonlight, as if a lantern dangled from the sky. Clear as day I could see Ma smiling.

"Let's hurry while your father's still asleep."

We unhooked our snowshoes from the eaves, then strapped them onto our feet. They were flat, in the shape of an oval, made from crisscrosses of sinew that would keep us from sinking in the snow.

Ma led us to a path above the river. Our steps were wide and clumsy, but we stayed atop the snowy crust, like three little birds.

Soon we saw steam rising into the air and smelled sulfur. There were no human footprints in any direction, so we knew we were alone. Quick, we took off every stitch of clothing, and folded it all under a tree where the pine needles were dry. Pinned up our hair. Standing bare-naked in the cold, my skin tingled.

Josie and I glanced at each other with a quiet giggle. Being naked wasn't regular to her either.

We stepped into the hot pool, the stones slippery with moss. I sunk in up to my chin. It was better than any bath: My whole self was instantly warm and there was room enough underwater to stretch my arms and legs. I looked over at Ma. In the moonlight she was more beautiful than ever, her golden hair coiled on top of her head, her neck graceful. I hoped someday to be as pretty.

The moon was rising. Every tree glistened, their boughs thick with snow. We spoke in whispers, to enjoy the quiet and not draw attention to ourselves. From the top of a nearby pine, an owl hooted. I could see its head swivel upon its square shoulders.

In the distance was a muffled beat from the stamp mills. Otherwise the forest was so still we heard only the water trickling from our hot spring down into the river.

"Girls, look." Ma pointed with her dripping hand to the pond below us some distance away. The moon shone on two sleeping swans, drifting together in a slow circle, just inches apart. Their long white necks were tucked under a wing behind them.

"Aren't they beautiful?" Ma whispered. "They mate for life, you know."

"Yes, Mama," I said. I wondered if she was thinking about Pa.

34
Winter

A few mornings later, we jumped awake. It was already seven o'clock! The windows were dark gray, no starlight or signs of dawn. Josie slid out of bed and felt her way to the door. She jiggled the latch, trying to push it open.

"Hallelujah!" she cried. "We're snowed in."

Ma hurried to the hearth to stir the coals into flames. "My word," she said, "we're late. The men'll be here soon, hungry like always."

"Ain't likely, Ma." Josie was now at the back door where Tall Sing had just appeared with a shovel. A low white tunnel led to his shed and the stable beyond. In the pale light I could see our horses eating from their manger.

"Yippee, there's about four feet of new snow, Ma. It'll take 'em hours to dig out the trail from town. We can be all by ourselves for a change."

Ma caught Josie as she twirled in her nightgown. "Chores first, my girl," said Ma. "We'll still get breakfast goin' for us and your Pa and whoever else might make their way here. There'll be time enough for dancing."

Our family had been snowed in plenty of times, but this was the biggest yet. I helped Tall Sing carve a path from our front door to the creek so we could break ice for fresh water. Then we climbed onto the roof. Together we pushed off as much snow as possible, down the back wall, so the ceiling wouldn't cave in. It was beautiful from up there. The sky was a brilliant blue, the sun so bright I had to squint. Every tree was frosted white, the hills too. The snow sparkled. Again, I could hear the faraway pounding of the stamp mills that never stopped for anything.

"How pretty," said Ma as she stood in the doorway, letting the sunlight touch her face. Drifts were over her head.

We looked toward town. If all of us didn't start digging, it would be spring before our customers could hike back and forth.

After breakfast, Pa harnessed the horses to a log six feet long. He turned the log sideways so it would roll behind them and help pack down the trail. He and Tall Sing stomped into the snow, Pa limping. They shoveled as much as they could, then urged the mares forward until it was too deep for them to continue. This they did again and again until a path began to emerge, firm enough to walk on without falling through the crust.

Meantime, I cleared the footbridge and swept it before the bottom layer could turn to ice. Ma gave Josie the job of scooping away the snow that covered our three windows. As soon as she did, the cabin was filled with light, and Ma blew out the lanterns.

"No need for these until tonight," she said, "Good work, Josie."

Just before noon we heard the distant ringing of sleigh bells.

"They're coming!" cried Josie.

Pa stopped to lean on his shovel, rubbing his swollen fingers. "Oh, it'll be a few hours yet, Josie girl. We'll keep goin' on our end and see where we all meet."

I felt hopeful knowing we weren't stranded. Of course every shelf of Ma's pantry was stocked, and we had plenty of smoked beef and hams hanging in Tall Sing's lean-to. It had been months since our family had been alone—by family I meant Tall Sing, too—and I liked how quiet things were, just the five of us. Pa's cheerfulness was a surprise. It reminded me of how he used to be—not just a day here, a day there, but all the time.

Josie was like a puppy with a waggedy-tail the way she ran around Pa wanting to help with the horses. Twice while he was leading the team forward she edged herself into his arms until he hugged her. She could always make him laugh, Josie could.

Pa was right. All through the sunny afternoon we could hear sleigh bells drawing nearer as we inched ahead through the drifts on our end. The mercury stood at three degrees above zero, but under the cloudless sky Josie and I got so warm we took off our cloaks and mittens.

As soon as the sun dipped behind the mountain, we heard cries of *hooray*. A team of prospectors with shovels and assorted mules and horses wearing bells in their harnesses broke through the final wall that had separated us from town. Even though the men looked dead tired and ready for a hot meal, they were whistling and singing like it was a holiday.

Pa showed them to our corral on the wide side of the river where they could rest their animals. He and Tall Sing had put out fresh hay and water, figuring there'd be a need.

The sight that made me happiest was Whiskey Nose riding his donkey. For some reason he had dressed Puddin'head in a lady's red bonnet with two holes cut out for its ears, a red ribbon tied under its gray chin. Maybe I just needed to laugh, but it was the funniest thing I'd seen in a long time, and laugh I did, Josie too.

From his saddle pack, Whiskey Nose pulled out an assortment of food we hadn't tasted since summer—dried figs, a round of cheese, and two boxes of salted herring—gifts for Ma.

"Been saving these for Christmas," he told her as he hauled everything in his good arm to our table, "but that's two weeks away, Mrs. Kidd. My motto is 'Give now,' 'cause who knows what'll happen tomorrow."

35
A Debt to Pay

Two days before Christmas, I was in the library. There was no stove for heat, but afternoon sunlight coming through its window warmed it up just enough. On account of the mountain passes being buried in snow, there'd been no Wells Fargo or other travelers for a couple weeks, so when I heard people cheering along Main Street I knew someone had managed to dig through.

Quick I set down the medical journal I'd been reading and flung open the door. Sure enough, a team of eight horses, their sleigh bells ringing in the cold air, was pulling a wagon piled high with boxes, crates, and bags—our long-awaited supplies. What a sight! Folks began pouring out of their stores and houses.

"Just in time for Santy Claus!" someone yelled.

The driver stopped in front of the mercantile, where several men helped him unload. Many hefted sacks over their shoulders and carried them to City Market and Poppy's Dry Goods, then to the bakery and butcher shop. When the driver continued on to the post office, he stopped where I was standing just long enough to throw four mailbags onto the sidewalk.

"I'll be leaving tomorrow morning at nine," he called from his high seat, "so tell folks there's time to write some letters." He looked up at the gray clouds gathering along the mountain range. "That is, if there ain't another blizzard." He clicked his tongue, turning his horses for the livery stable at the edge of town.

The bags were too heavy for me to lift, so one by one I rolled them inside. By then a small crowd had gathered, among them Judge Reno. He looked dapper in his black frock coat and top hat, a wool scarf around his neck, but I did not like the smile he gave me. It was too friendly. We'd only met the one time, at the Fourth of July picnic.

To the crowd I said, "Please come back at three o'clock. By then I'll have most of this sorted. Thanks, everyone. Whiskey Nose is still recuperating."

When the judge didn't leave with the others, I said, "Let me see if you have mail from last time." I turned to look in the R slot, but he put his hand on my arm.

"That's not why I'm here, dear."

I brushed his hand away. "What is it then?"

"There's a matter concerning your father."

My heart started racing. Pa and I had eaten breakfast together before I'd gone to town. Maybe something had happened since then. "Is he all right?" I asked.

"Well," he said, "not entirely."

I hid my hands in the folds of my skirt so he wouldn't see me shaking. Looking right at him, I said, "Go on."

"Your father is in debt. Don't get me wrong, he's good at the game, but lately he's been losing more than he wins. As a result, he owes several of us money."

"How much?"

"A considerable sum, young lady."

"Meaning?"

The judge reached into his vest pocket where the gold chain of his watch was looped around a button. He unfolded a piece of paper.

"For starters," he said, glancing at the penciled numbers, "five hundred dollars to Shorty. That's for the beer and sandwiches he buys for everyone twice a week. There's no argument that your father is generous."

"Five *hundred*?" That was a fortune. Why would Pa buy food when we had plenty at home?

"That's right. Then, not too long ago, he bet several of the boys at Dog Face Sam's fifty bucks each in a wrestling match. As you might suspect, he lost. There's three hundred right there."

I felt stricken. How would Pa ever repay this? And why was he betting money he didn't have? It was more than Ma and I had ever earned or even laid eyes on.

"Last but not least," he continued, "he owes me one thousand, one hundred, ninety-six dollars. A personal loan to help him out of his many scrapes. Total is one thousand, nine hundred and ninety-six, just a few bucks shy of two grand."

My hands were still in my skirt, but I was getting mad. "Why are you telling me this, Judge?"

"Your father loves his family. I'd loathe for him to end up in the calaboose or worse, if you know what I mean." He put his manicured fingers to his scarf, straightening it.

"I don't know what you mean."

But I did. Pa could find himself with a noose around his neck, courtesy of his friends the vigilantes. I stared hard at Judge Reno until he glanced away. He cleared his throat.

"What I'm trying to tell you, dear girl, is that if you and your lovely mother pay me just twenty dollars a week, I'll see to it that the fellas calm down. It'll buy your father some time, is what I'm getting at."

"I thought you and my pa were friends."

"A debt is a debt," he answered.

I did some quick figures in my head. "Twenty dollars a week. If we can even come up with that much, it would take near two years to pay it off."

Judge Reno shrugged. "Tell you what. Each time you come to town, bring what you can to my office. It'll give me and you a chance to become better acquainted."

36

Into the Night

While we were fixing supper, I told Ma about Judge Reno's visit to the post office. She lowered herself onto a stool, her hands on the table.

"Two . . . thousand . . . dollars?" she whispered.

We could see out the window to where Pa was carrying an armful of firewood, limping with slow steps. In the waning sunlight he was smiling at Josie, who held a bird's nest in her palm. She had showed it to us earlier, after finding it beneath a branch that had snapped in the wind. To watch them together, if felt like the prettiest of days.

"What're we going to do, Ma?"

"I am thinking on it, Clementine."

Supper wasn't the same now that I knew Pa's predicament. *Our* predicament. Shorty was more quiet than regular. So were the other fellas. I didn't care what Jesse Blue thought, him being a snake and all. But I wondered if the judge had told them about our talk, and were they expecting payment soon? Or maybe they were uneasy on account they were our friends.

Whatever the reasons, I could barely keep myself from pacing the floor as our customers took their time finishing their pie and second cups of coffee. Only when each had put on his hat for the walk home did I feel I could breathe again.

But instead of clearing dishes from the table right away, I went over to the fire. Pa was in the rocking chair, rubbing his knees.

"What is it, darlin'?"

I looked over at the pantry where Ma was setting the lid on our cracker barrel. With a nod she signaled that I should answer him.

"Papa, Judge Reno came to me." Then I described the conversation.

Pa looked at me with sorry eyes. "I *told* Judge I'd pay, but he doesn't believe me. What kind of man threatens my daughter? A coward, that's who!"

"I have some ideas, Papa."

"So do I, darlin'. There's a game tonight at Shorty's, a big one. I'll win it, you just wait and see."

"Not tonight, Papa!" Josie cried. "I saw snow clouds over the mountain. Stay here with us."

"I got to do it, girls." He grabbed his six-shooter from the mantel and strapped it around his waist. Then he went for his coat, putting his arms through the sleeves as he walked out the door.

Ma rushed across the room. "Dallas," she cried, "don't go. We'll find a way to help you!" She stood in the doorway calling after him as cold air filled our cabin. But her voice met silence. I came to her side. We could see Pa limp across the river and reach the trail for town. A rising full moon would light his way.

When at last Ma closed the door, she leaned against it, her hand over her heart like to slow its beating. "Clementine, I can't let him get into another game. Chances are he'll lose again and lose big and our family will be in even deeper trouble." She turned up the wick on one of our lanterns, then took her cloak from its hook.

"Let me go, Ma," I said. "I can run faster than you."

She looked at Josie, who had worked her way under my arm, then leaned over to kiss both of us. "Thank you, darlin', but he's my husband. He needs me."

It grew late. By nine o'clock when Ma hadn't returned, I figured she and Pa would eventually come home together. I read to Josie from *Peter Parley's Book of Fables* until she fell asleep, then got up to put another log on the fire. Poked the coals so it would burn slow through the night. Blew out the candle.

It was too cold to wait outside, and I didn't want Josie to get scared if she woke to find herself alone. I peered out the window that faced the trail. No sign of Ma's lantern.

At last I crawled under our warm quilt, determined to keep my eyes open, but the next thing I knew it was three in the morning. I heard the chiming of the clock and the door latch shut. Quiet steps into Ma and Pa's room. Too tired to even open my eyes I waited for the familiar creak of their bed before letting myself fall back to sleep.

37
Christmas Eve

The cabin was cold when I awoke at dawn. Josie was still asleep, so I slipped out of bed to get the fire going. It wasn't like Ma not to be up already, but I figured she was tired from last night.

On account it was Christmas Eve, I decided to get breakfast started. Customers would be coming in another hour. At the sound of pots sliding onto the iron stove, Josie peeked out from her covers.

"Mornin', Clementine," she said.

"Morning to you, sleepyhead." I smiled over at her. In a bound she ran to our parents' room to wake them up, a tradition whenever there was a holiday.

I was peeling strips of bacon off its slab and placing them in the skillet when she leaned out of their room.

"Is Ma outside at the privy?" she asked.

"No, I'm the first one—" But I stopped midsentence and turned to look at her. "What d'you mean, Josie?"

"Ma ain't here. Just Pa."

I pushed the skillet to the back of the stove and wiped my hands on my apron.

"Not here?" I hurried over. Pa was dead asleep, his arm around Ma's pillow. I rushed to the pantry, then to each window, pulling aside the curtains.

"Ma?" I cried. "Mother!"

Tall Sing came in the back door.

"Ma's not here, Tall Sing. Have you seen her?" Without waiting for an answer I ran outside. Nearly a foot of new snow had fallen in the night, and there were no prints leading to the outhouse or anywhere else. Not one. I raced around the cabin to the front. Same thing. Just tiny tracks from birds and a rabbit.

There was no sign of our mother.

I stormed back inside and into their bedroom. "Pa?" I shook his shoulder, hard. Then harder. "Wake up, Pa!"

Josie appeared with a cup of icy water and threw it in his face. He sputtered awake and sat up good and mad. "What the—"

"Where's our mother?" Josie asked.

Pa rubbed his hand through his wet hair. His eyes were bloodshot. "What?"

"She went to town to get you," I said. "Didn't you come home together?"

Pa's brow creased. He shook his head, still not understanding. "What're you talking about? What happened?"

"I'm asking *you* what happened." Terror was in the pit of my stomach so deep I feared I would start screaming. My mother would never leave us. Never. And she wouldn't have stayed overnight in town without sending word that she was all right. Something terrible had happened to her, I just knew it.

Pa sat on the end of his bed. "Girls, I didn't see your mother in town. Honest. Someone would've told me if she was there." He looked at me, questions in his eyes, pleading for me to explain. "You mean she came after me? To Shorty's?"

"Yes!" I shouted.

At that Josie started wailing. Tall Sing drew us out of Pa's room to sit by the fire. He kept his hand on our shoulders while my sister and I sobbed. Ma had gone into the night with only her cloak and lantern. If she fell or got lost, the cold would've seized her, or a mountain lion. And now that more snow had fallen, it would be impossible to find her tracks.

After some moments, Pa came to us on unsteady feet. He held his hands to his head. "Where is she then, Clementine?"

Josie flew at our father, pounding her fists against his chest. "How can you go to bed and not notice your wife ain't right beside you? You were drunk again, weren't you?"

My mind felt crazy with worry and solutions. "We've got to start searching right now," I said, going out the door for my snowshoes.

"Clemmy." Tall Sing's voice was calm. He led me back into the cabin. "You could get lost. Let the men search. They coming now, see? You and Josie cook, give 'em good pancakes and bacon."

Tall Sing turned away, but I had seen the look in his eyes. He was worried, too.

38
Searching

All Christmas Eve, Pa and our friends searched up and down Gold Digger's Canyon. They tromped over the new snow but could not find any sign of my mother, not a snag of cloth on a bush or her lantern. Nothing. Josie and I stayed in the cabin with Tall Sing, minding a kettle of soup on the stove and keeping the coffee hot.

To distract myself I rolled out dough for biscuits, dozens and dozens, more than we needed, but I couldn't stop. Seemed if I could stay busy, time would go faster and someone would find Ma, cold but alive. When Boone burst in through the door with snow on his boots, I let myself fall into his arms. He held me like a gentleman.

Meantime, customers and townsfolk came to warm up and fill their bellies in between their searchings. Each one had a theory. They were polite and concerned when they knew I could hear their conversations, but soon as I stepped into the pantry, their whispers began.

On purpose I tarried at the shelves, wanting to catch what they were saying. But their words only made it worse.

She run off, sure as shootin'.

Dry Boots Kidd ain't no peach, it's no wonder she skedaddled.
Bet she had a boyfriend.

Probably took that last stage out of town. It was the Full
Moon Express, you know, down into Boise City.

Shhh.

When they saw me coming back to the table, they
cleared their throats. I set a platter of pickles, cheese, and
herring in front of them, part of what Ma had planned for our
Christmas dinner. No one met my eye.

How could they say such things about Ma? They didn't
know her like I did. They discussed the Lester boys, how
their mother disappeared in the middle of the night, no
farewell to her sons or husband, just a note tacked to the
Wells Fargo office: "Cain't take it no more. Betty Lester."

And there were other women who had deserted their
families, the men reminded one another. I shut my ears.
Boone, kind Boone, said nothing.

In the quiet hours of Christmas night while Josie whimpered
in her sleep, Pa sat by the fire, his rocker creaking over the
stones. His eyes were open but not seeing, like the doomed
elk. I crept into Ma's room and went through her trunk.
Searching for clues, I found only linens and her summer
dress, a tiny sewing box. All seemed regular. She didn't keep
a diary, so there was no way to guess what may have been
weighing on her mind.

What had she meant when she said Josie and I might
have to take care of ourselves someday? Did she mean now?

Had she planned on leaving Pa once I was being courted, with a husband in my future? And had she planned her get-away knowing a stage would travel under the full moon?

I kept my questions to myself.

But Pa couldn't stay quiet. "She was mad at me, wasn't she?" he raged at his friends the next morning. "I tried hard to make her happy. Why would she leave us?"

I reckoned the only way Pa could face losing my beautiful mother was to believe she had fled.

"When's Ma coming home?" Josie asked our father every day.

"Don't know, Josie honey." Pa tried to hug her, but she pushed him away by crossing her arms.

"It's all your fault, Pa!"

As for the poker game the night Ma went after him? Pa came home with empty pockets. At least his six-shooter was still loaded, which meant he hadn't shot anyone, thank God.

Ma's work fell to Josie and me. Our cold winter days went like this:

Josie helped me cook breakfast and clean. After our customers left, I escorted her to school, as she refused to let Pa. He limped along behind us, not knowing what to do with himself. I then opened up the library and post office for a few hours, while he came inside with me to keep warm. Two o'clock, I fetched Josie from school, Pa following.

One afternoon when she and I were hurrying home to start supper, Josie stopped on the trail. It was at the creek bend where we had seen those two elk struggling. She turned around to look at Pa. I expected her to scowl, but instead she smiled at him.

"Come on, Papa, we'll wait for you."

A few minutes later, we ran into Whiskey Nose on his donkey—we had heard him coughing from way back. Anyhow, he was hauling a sack of flour for us, and one of dried apples. Up ahead we came to Shorty and Jesse Blue. They each carried a box of herring and some coffee beans. At the cabin I took out my pouch of coins to pay them, but they turned their hands palm-down.

"You don't owe us nothin', Miss Clementine."

One morning, I left Pa in the library and trudged to the stage office in snow above my knees. The clerk looked up from his desk when I came in.

"Help you, miss?"

"Could you please check your passenger lists for December twenty-third, the last stage out of town?" I stomped the snow from my boots while brushing it off my skirt.

"Certainly." He pulled a ledger from a shelf and flipped through the pages. While he put a pair of spectacles to his nose and squinted, I read the notes pinned on the wall. To my relief, there was nothing in Ma's handwriting.

"Here we are, miss." He used his thumb to hold his place, then turned the notebook so I could see for myself.

My eyes scanned the sheet. Six passengers had boarded the Full Moon Express for Boise City, but only five were listed. On the sixth line where it said "Name and occupation," the clerk had written, "Female. Prefers to remain anonymous."

I took a breath. "This woman," I pointed. "Can you describe her?"

He gazed out the window. After a moment he said, "Lots of folks come and go, you understand. But as I recollect, her hood obscured her face. Didn't have any luggage, seemed in a hurry. That's about it, miss."

I kept this information to myself. I couldn't believe that Ma had abandoned us, but now there was a question.

39

The Rescuer

Even though Josie was upset, our mother's disappearance began to bring out the best in her. Every night after sweeping up after supper, she took an oil lamp to the table to do her schoolwork.

"Ma would be so proud of you," I told her.

But as for Pa, he got worse. He spent more time in the saloons, and when he came home he moped by the hearth, leaving the firewood and other man chores to Tall Sing.

One evening while our customers were finishing their pie and putting coins under their plates, Pa lunged across the table and grabbed Jesse Blue by the throat.

"You no good thief," Pa said. "I seen how you made eyes at my wife. It's 'cause of you she took off."

Now, I held no high opinion of Jesse Blue, but I was worried for his very life at the stranglehold Pa had. He struck at Pa's arms, trying to free himself with one hand and draw his gun with the other, but Pa wouldn't let go. I looked around the room for someone to jump in and help before my father got himself shot. It seemed the men were as startled as I was. Meantime, cups, saucers, and spoons clattered to the floor as Pa climbed onto the table to get a better grip on Jesse Blue.

"Stop it, Pa!" I screamed, hitting him on his back. "Not in Ma's house. You can't do this. Stop!"

He turned on me so fast I barely had time to jump aside. There was murder in his eyes, I swear it. The same as that night when he stabbed our pillows. I had been afraid of him then and I was afraid of him now.

"You knew all along, didn't you, Clementine?"

"Please stop," I said again. "Ma loved you, Papa, no one else. She was devoted to you. Never complained, never said an unkind word about you." I signaled to Josie to run outside, to safety.

"Then why'd she leave, huh?"

I gave no answer. He'd been in town drinking all day. Ma's words came to me like a quiet voice in my head: "Only fools argue with drunks." Pa grabbed my arms.

I twisted to get out of his grasp but he was too strong. Jesse Blue, meantime, was getting up from the table, trying to shake his head clear, to come to my aid. Even Whiskey Nose began beating at Pa with his good arm, coughing something terrible from his effort. Customers who had started to leave were coming back in the door.

But before any of them could do anything, I felt Pa being torn away from me and lifted into the air. In one swoop some-one wrestled him to the floor, facedown, then tied his arms behind his back with rope. Everything happened so fast, it took a moment before I realized my rescuer was Tall Sing. His old face was calm, but I could see his anger.

Oh no, I thought. Tall Sing would be punished for sure.

But Tall Sing didn't seem worried. He saw me rubbing my arms where Pa had wrenched me.

"Clemmy?" His eyebrows were raised in a question.

"I'm all right, Tall Sing."

It seemed the room froze. No one spoke. Even my sister was calm.

Jesse Blue broke the silence by pulling Pa to his feet and dragging him to the hearth, where he shoved him into the rocker. Quick as an inch he drew his revolver from his holster and pressed the barrel against Pa's cheek.

"Dallas Kidd," he said, "you and I been friends since Californie, but you ever touch your daughters, I personally will shoot you in that thick head of yours. Ain't a man here who won't do the same." Jesse Blue looked around before putting his gun away. The others were nodding, but they also were doing a curious thing that near brought me to tears.

They were picking up the remainder of our dinner, all the plates, cups, and coins that Pa had made a mess of, stacking them on the table. Shorty took the broom and swept the spilled cobbler into the fire, ignoring Pa sitting there in his chair.

Josie rushed from the doorway to help. "Oh fellas, thank you so much, but this ain't your job. Here, I'll take that."

Our cabin was clean before I knew it and our customers bid us goodnight. All, that is, except Whiskey Nose and Jesse Blue. They asked for blankets to sleep by the fire.

"Ain't gonna leave you girls alone till we know he's sober," they said.

They hauled Pa to bed, then tied his hands in front of him. Took off his boots and covered him with Ma's quilt. He was out cold before the rest of us turned in.

I was badly shaken by Pa's attack, especially on account Ma wasn't there like last time, to soothe us, to defend us. Josie and I tucked ourselves into bed behind our curtain, then I read to her by a short candle.

Only when I blew it out did a sudden thought bring me comfort: Pa had no idea a Chinaman had thrown him to the ground. And after seeing the looks on our friends' faces, I reckoned he never would.

40
Great Expectations

While I grieved for Ma, not knowing if she was dead or had run away, I tried to reason what she would want me to do.

Some facts I couldn't ignore: One, Pa's bad days were getting worse. He was dangerous and it was up to me to make sure Josie and I were safe. Two, his debts were beyond anything I could ever pay. The thought of facing Judge Reno on this subject made me sick.

The third thing was Boone had asked Pa for my hand in marriage.

Pa said, "Why, of course, son, the sooner the better." But I had not given an answer. Our courtship was crowded on account of my being so busy and not wanting to leave Josie alone with our father.

I had to start making plans.

One day when Josie was at school and Pa in town, I went to the shed where Ma had hidden her money in the chimney. Removed the brick and lifted out the leather pouch. It was much heavier with coins than when she had shown it to me before. The last thing Ma would've wanted was for Pa to discover the money she had saved for us and then lose it all in a poker game.

There was only one better place to hide it.

The snow was still deep. I hiked upriver, then doubled back on a higher path that looked like a deer trail, but I knew the narrow footprints were Tall Sing's. This was his secret way to his cabin. When I climbed the steep gulley I was careful to stay away from where the abandoned mine shafts lay hidden.

Soon I saw a curl of smoke rising in the air above the chokecherry shrubs. I ducked under the branches that hid his cabin from the trail and raised my hand to knock on the door.

I was surprised to hear an unfamiliar voice coming from inside.

"... *Miss Havisham was taking exercise,*" the voice said, "*in the room with the long spread table, leaning on her crutch stick. The room was lighted as of yore, and at the sound of our entrance, she stopped and turned. She was then just abreast of the rotted bride-cake....*"

Right away I knew someone was reading from "Great Expectations," by Charles Dickens, a serial Ma had read to Josie and me from a New York newspaper. It had become our favorite story. I would never forget the character of Miss Havisham and her ruined wedding.

I knocked. The voice stopped. From inside came the sound of rustling and a chair being moved. Tall Sing opened the door.

"Come in, Clemmy."

Cautious, I stepped inside. No one else was there. Heat radiated from his tiny stove, where there was a teapot and a bowl of rice.

"Was that you reading?" I asked him.

He laughed. "Who else?" Stooping so as not to bump his head on the low ceiling, he motioned me to a bench near his table. "Sit down, dear, it is time we had a talk."

My jaw must have dropped. He had been reading perfectly and now was speaking perfectly, with only a slight accent. I was stunned. "How—"

"Clemmy," he said, "when you were a baby, your mother taught me how to read English and pronounce it correctly. She assured me that if I would read aloud to myself every day I would be able to communicate as well as any educated American."

I was still bewildered.

Tall Sing's face creased into a smile. "There are people who think foreigners with big accents are stupid, that they cannot think or solve problems. When your parents hired me as a servant, I didn't let your father see me reading the books your mother gave me. Imagine. He would have called me uppity and sent me away. And I would not be here today for you and Josie."

"I'm glad you never left, Tall Sing." I paused. "But what about your own little girls?" This question had been bothering me since I had seen that lonely doll the last time I was there.

"Ah."

We sat quietly for several moments, both of us looking out the window. When at last he answered, his eyes were moist.

"This was many years ago," he began. "I was tending to a mother and new baby in a hillside hut when I heard screams from my village on the shore below. I ran to the edge of the cliff and looked down. I could see blue ocean and the small island where my brothers liked fishing for octopus. But my village had disappeared. The beach and houses and shops were covered with churning water. A giant wave had swept in from the sea and washed everything away. Everything."

Tall Sing looked at me. "And everyone," he said. "My wife and two daughters, who had been grilling our morning fish over a fire. My brothers, who had been mending their nets on shore. My parents and sister. All our neighbors and friends. Some days later I found An May's doll in a tree. But that's all I found, Clemmy."

I glanced at the doll, feeling tears in my throat. "Is that why you came to America?"

"Yes. To start new."

"I'm sorry, Tall Sing."

He reached over to pat my hand. "Watching you and Josie grow up has helped, my dear. I was not looking for a new family, but that is what I found."

The cabin was quiet except for the hiss of coals in his stove. He pointed to Ma's pouch in my lap. "May I presume you need a good hiding place for that?"

I handed it to him.

He went to the corner under his bunk, lifted a small

piece of floorboard, then pressed the bag into the dirt below it. "It will be safe here."

While he poured tea into small porcelain cups and gave me one, I looked around the room at his collection of bottles and jars and the herbs hanging overhead. His mortar and pestle prompted my next question.

I held the cup of steaming tea below my chin. It smelled good, like mint and ginger.

"Tall Sing, will you help me cure Pa of the drinking and gambling sickness? Maybe we can make him better if we find the right medicine."

He took a slow sip of tea.

"There is no medicine for these things. It is a matter of the human spirit. Your papa must *want* to be well."

When Tall Sing saw I was trying to hold back tears, he patted my hand again. "Do you know why your parents named you Clementine?"

I shook my head.

"It means 'merciful one.' They hoped you would grow in that virtue. And you have, my dear."

41

Birthday Ribbons

My days at the post office became personal. I searched through every letter and parcel in hopes of finding something from Ma. I wanted to believe she was still alive and would send word.

I also read every line of every newspaper from San Francisco to Boise City to Salt Lake, again in hopes there might be mention of a woman starting up her own bookstore or library, something Ma might do if she was out on her own. It was possible, I kept telling myself. Anything was possible.

One ad in particular caught my eye, but for a different reason.

> TWO POSITIONS AVAILABLE May 1867: Clean, respectable boardinghouse seeks **YOUNG LADY** to be a companion for six-year-old girl in exchange for room and board. **COOK** needed, Caucasian preferred, Chinese may apply. See Mrs. Christianson, 8th and Pueblo Sts., Boise City.

That very moment I took pencil and paper and wrote Mrs. Christianson about Josie, about our mother, and about Tall Sing being a doctor *and* a cook. I knew this was all right with him, since the last time we talked, he said he would help me with Josie in any way possible.

No sooner had I blown the ink dry on my letter than the stage arrived for pickup. It would be an eight-hour drive down the mountain, so I knew my request might be delivered the next morning, possibly even read over afternoon tea.

My reckoning was this: If I could get Josie away from Pa, away from this wild mining camp, there was a better chance of her staying out of trouble and more likely she'd become the civilized girl our mother dreamed for her. And if Tall Sing also worked for Mrs. Christianson, then I could sleep at night. He would watch over her like she was his own daughter.

As for myself, my affection for Boone was growing. One thing for certain, he would not take any nonsense from Pa if he went crazy again. The way he had protected Tall Sing, I knew Boone would protect me, too.

But I no longer wanted to live up Gold Digger's Canyon, even though Boone was building a cabin intended for us. It was lonely on the mountain, and winters were rough. I was tired of life around gamblers and vigilantes. Tired of worrying about my father.

I told our customers that on the following Tuesday—Josie's birthday—I would not be serving their usual supper. Instead, I would be taking her and Pa to dinner in town, at the Western Café. It was to be the first time my sister or I had ever eaten in a restaurant.

Boone was arranging a special gift for her. What with all the heartache and commotion at Christmas, there had been no happy surprises, and the New Year of 1867 began without a single cheer from any of us. My seventeenth birthday had come and gone without notice.

I was six years old the day Josie was born. We lived up a canyon in Miners Creek, California. By the time the midwife arrived at our cabin, Tall Sing had already helped Ma deliver my baby sister. My parents named her Josie, for "joy."

Now she was eleven, becoming a young lady right before my eyes. As we sat in the café at the little square table with Pa, I felt proud of my sister.

"Josie, Ma would be mighty pleased that you're reading Charles Dickens on your own."

"I know," she said.

"And I'm sure Ma would compliment you on your hair. I sure like it."

Josie grinned. Instead of two pigtails like regular, she had made seven braids that hung below her shoulders, a different colored ribbon tied on each end—blue, green, red, yellow, orange, violet, and pink. These ribbons were Pa's birthday gift to her.

Still smiling, she shook her head for a swirl of rainbow.

"Josie, honey, I like your style," said Pa. He lifted his spoon, careful not to spill soup on the white tablecloth. He was wearing a blue shirt and string tie, his rugged face clean-shaven. These past months I had forgotten my father was a handsome man. That morning he went to the barbershop for a trim after I offered to pay. Instead of giving Pa the fifty cents, though, I handed it to the barber himself so my father would not stop at the saloon first.

I wish Ma had been with us in the café, to see Pa at his gentle best, and Josie sitting up straight, using her fork like a lady. Not once did my sister cuss, and each time she used the word *ain't*, she stopped to correct herself.

While the waiter cleared our plates and served us each a chunk of chocolate cake, I kept glancing out the window for Boone. Soon he appeared on the sidewalk, a small bundle in his arms.

I hoped that when Josie saw her present, she would be brave with what Pa and I were about to tell her.

And I had an announcement of my own.

42

Dead Eyes

Mrs. Christianson's letter had arrived so fast it was like the Pony Express was back in business. She was a lonely widow, delighted to hear about Josie and Tall Sing, and said they could move in as soon as convenient. My sister would share a room with the little girl, Libby, and Tall Sing would sleep in the carriage house with the gardener and stable man.

At first I was nervous about telling Pa that Josie was moving away, but when I did he seemed relieved. I poured him a cup of coffee, then sat down next to him.

"Don't hardly know what to do now with your ma gone," he said. "Maybe it'll be better for Josie to get a fresh start." His voice was so low I had to lean close to hear him. "Clementine, I thought me and Judge Reno were friends, but he says we gotta come up with the cash soon or else."

"Papa, don't worry." I lay my head on his shoulder. "We'll figure something out."

* * *

When Boone pulled up a chair at Josie's birthday dinner and set a bundle on the table, was she ever surprised. It was a scrap of blanket bunched up like a nest.

"Guess what we got you, Josie girl." Boone lifted a flap of cloth and bent close to it. "Hello?" he said to something moving inside. "Ready to meet your new mistress?"

"What's in there?" Josie cried, nearly knocking over her glass of milk as she strained to see. "Show me, please?"

Boone opened the blanket. There sat a yellow kitten, purring so loud a woman at the next table looked over with a smile.

"Oh, Clementine. Is it for me, really?"

"Yes, honey. Happy birthday. From all of us."

Josie scooped up the kitten and held it to her chest. With her finger she pet the tiny head. "Thank you, oh thank you. I love her already. Thanks, Papa and Boone."

"Got a name for 'er?" asked Pa.

"Hmm." Josie closed her eyes for a moment. "I'm a-thinkin' on it," she said.

My sister was sounding more like Ma each day.

"Josie," I said, "Papa and I have another surprise for you."

"Yippee! What kind?"

"An adventure—"

But before I could tell her, a gunshot shattered the café window, spewing glass over the front tables. Josie and I were back far enough that we didn't get cut, but right away I knew the lady next to us needed a doctor.

That was only half of it.

An instant after the glass exploded, a man landed on our table—*our* table—with such force it collapsed. His dead eyes stared up at the ceiling, his revolver still in his holster. Blood seeped from the front of his shirt, growing a red puddle beneath him. I scooted as far away from him as possible—dragging Josie with me—sickened by the sight of him, and his stink. He smelled about as full of whiskey as any man could get.

Quick as a shout, Pa and Boone hustled out the door after the gunman. I reckoned they were most mad that the bullet could've killed one of us instead.

The poor lady's husband was yelling for help. I rushed over and pulled off their tablecloth, making even more of a mess as their dinner crashed to the floor.

"Tear this into strips," I instructed him.

The woman was sitting in her chair, her white high-collared blouse stained with blood. I took her hand in mine and in a calm voice said, "You'll be all right, ma'am, just hold still."

She was bleeding from shards in her neck, cheek, and down her left arm, and was trying to catch her breath, such was her shock. How I wished I could calm her by saying I was a doctor, but for now I would just have to do what Tall Sing had been teaching me.

First, I tore her sleeve from the wrist up to her shoulder, to examine her wounds. Then careful as could be, I put my fingers to the splinters and pulled each one out, dropping them into a pile beside me. Thirty-four, I counted.

Meantime, the cook had brought over an oil lamp and

was holding it high so I could see better. Someone else gave me a flask of whiskey after I called for some.

"Press the cloth here . . . ," I told her husband, "and here. Good. Now, sir, dab the cuts with this alcohol. It'll sting, but it'll do its work. Then give her a few swigs of it so she'll sleep easy. Ma'am, you look fine and probably won't need stitches, but if it's all right with your husband, I'll have Tall Sing check on you anyhow."

While I tended to her, the café owner and his brother dragged the dead man by his boots out to the sidewalk. His body left a long red smear and a crowd of folks staring at it.

I glanced around for Josie and was glad to see some patrons keeping her off to the side. Her kitten was a yellow fluff in her arm. It was on my mind that we still needed to tell her about Mrs. Christianson.

But for now, that and my announcement would have to wait.

43

The Offer

In bed that night Josie and I whispered so as not to wake Pa, her kitten asleep on the pillow between us. After I explained everything, she was quiet.

"Josie?"

Big sigh.

"What're you thinking, honey?"

She sighed again. "I'll be glad to help Mrs. Christianson, but I won't be glad to leave you. When you and Boone get married, won't you please move down to the valley so we can see each other regular?"

"Josie, I haven't said yes to Boone. Right now I'm worried about Papa. He's in some trouble and I want to help. Maybe it'll all be figured out by the time school's over, just a couple weeks away."

My sister closed her eyes. In the candlelight I saw a tear slide down her cheek. "Clementine, do you think Ma'll ever come back?"

"With all my soul I hope she does. Now go to sleep, Josie

girl. Your day has been bigger than most." It troubled me that she had said nothing about the murdered man landing on her birthday cake. Like she'd grown to expect such terrible things.

By the stroke of midnight I was still awake, watching the firelight dim. Wind moaned in the eaves. I had decided to visit Judge Reno on the morrow, to tell him that with Ma gone it would take forever to come up with near two thousand dollars. Maybe he'd hire me for his office and would help Pa find a job so together we could work off the debt. I knew of no other way.

The trail was white with an inch of fresh snow, not enough to slow our trek into town. Cold sunshine was rising through the forest, casting ragged shadows across our path. My stomach twisted with dread knowing I would soon see Judge Reno. After escorting Josie to school, I sorted the latest mail.

A boy came in and slapped a letter on the counter. "For you," he said, before running outside.

For one frozen moment I thought—hoped—it was a message from my mother. But after breaking the wax seal and unfolding the stationery, I realized the handwriting wasn't hers.

Dearest Clementine: I'll be brief. If you agree to become Mrs. Reno, I will remove all of your father's debts with one stroke of my pen. A happy solution for both our families. Eager for your reply in the affirmative, Judge L.H.R.

I was so stunned, I had to lean against the wall to steady myself. Read it three times to make sure I understood.

A reverse dowry was what it was. A bride for the judge's son, a gift for my father. Everyone knew that LeRoy and Boone were not close. Rumor was that the judge wanted Boone to marry a local girl, someone who wouldn't mind staying in Nugget. A cheerful daughter-in-law would help father and son become friends. At least that's what folks were saying.

Anyhow, as I looked out at the snow it seemed the judge's offer was a miracle. I would not have to worry about Pa disappearing in the night at the hand of vigilantes. It would give him a chance to get back on his feet.

Best of all were my true feelings for Boone. They had deepened over the past weeks, and at Josie's birthday dinner my answer had been ready: *I'll be glad and proud to marry you, Boone.* But of course, that moment had been lost.

I left a note on the post office door saying I would return at noon.

During winter every pool hall and street corner was crowded with loafers; that is, men and boys who had stopped their prospecting until the rivers weren't so thick with ice. As I headed toward Third Street I passed two Chinese carrying baskets of laundry over their shoulders. Some boys were running alongside them, squinting and mocking their language by talking fast jibberish.

This time I hurried on.

At the Renos' house, I opened the picket gate and

walked up the path. The judge was alone at his desk, smoking his pipe.

"Dear girl, how nice to see you." He stood up to take my cloak.

"I'll only be a moment," I said.

"Are you sure you won't let me take your wrap? Stay for a cup of tea?"

"Thank you anyway. I only came to say that I accept your offer and I am happy to marry Boone."

He took a long draw on his pipe, then leaned back in his chair. "Clementine dear," he said, with an odd smile, "I wasn't talking about you marrying *Boone.*"

44

Thinking on Things

Judge Reno's words silenced me like a shotgun.

I watched his face for a sign that he'd been joking, but his eyes were studying me, from my neck down to my ankles. With a slow gaze he was taking me in, same as the gamblers and drunks had done in Shorty's Saloon.

When I tried to speak, my voice was just a whisper. "Your son and I are courting but you want me to marry *you?*"

He nodded.

I ran out the door.

I ran through town and up Gold Digger's Canyon. Several times I slipped in the slush, but I kept going, reeling with a sick knowledge. All these months while Boone had been wooing me and winning my heart, his father had plans of his own.

I reached our cabin in a burst of tears. Pacing in front of the fireplace, I cried, "Ma, what should I do? I need you!"

Tall Sing appeared at the back door. I rushed into his arms and cried like I had as a ten-year-old when our dog drowned in the river. I told him everything. Then he made me sit at the table. He put herbs into a teapot and filled it with steaming water from our kettle, the one we always kept warm on the stove.

"Clemmy, what are you going to do?"

My head hurt. My lungs ached from running up the canyon without stopping to rest.

"You know I will help you," he said when I didn't answer.

"Thank you, Tall Sing." Josie's kitten jumped into my lap, rubbing her head against my hand so I would pet her. Her purring was a comfort.

We took our tea outside where the sun warmed the bench against the front of our cabin, the kitten stretched out between us. Ice along the sunny side of the creek was beginning to puddle. How quick winter was coming to its end. Near noon I remembered my note on the post office door.

"Tall Sing, I have to get back to work. Do you have any errands in town? We could walk together." I had some ponderings to share with him. A new plan.

Be wise, was Ma's voice in my head. *Take things slow, Clementine. Think.*

That afternoon I wrote a note to Judge Reno and gave it to a boy who was playing hooky. Paid him fifty cents in silver, then when he ran back with the judge's signature on a piece of paper, I gave him another fifty cents. My message was brief.

To the Honorable Judge Reno, Territory of Idaho:

Please forgive me for leaving your office this morning without further conversation. I am considering your generous offer. Thank you for being patient with me.

Yours sincerely, Clementine Kidd

For the next two hours I tended to the mail, greeting townsfolk like everything was regular. Some were still talking about the shooting at the Western Café. So far the murderer was on the loose, and the victim's body was in a shed waiting for the cemetery to thaw.

Meantime, I was thinking on things. I recollected the grizzly Ma and I had seen last summer, how we stepped away from it slow and quiet. Hid in the trees and waited. I also thought about the elk, how careful I had to be with my aim, to untangle their antlers and free them. There were lessons for me from these wild animals.

When Josie's class was dismissed for the day, she walked by herself to the library. She helped me sweep, then she wrote her name on the checkout list for the new *Harper's Weekly*. I felt cheered by her four braids and the ribbons she had tied on their ends: blue, purple, red, and white. She was the only girl I knew with such gumption.

We were halfway home where the trail narrows along the river when Josie handed me her lunch pail and the *Harper's*.

"Lookie there," she said, stepping off the path. She reached into a melting snowdrift where the dark shape of a horseshoe could be seen. When she tried to pick it up, it turned out to be a large iron ring. And it was attached to something buried in the snow.

We stared a moment, wondering, then I crouched next to her. Together we dug at the object.

Josie had found the handle to a lantern.

45

The Lantern

In the calmest voice I ever heard Josie use, she said, "It's Ma's, ain't it?"

My heart beat wildly as I lifted the lantern. Its sides were of speckled tin, the kind that would cast a lacy light from its candle. The kind of pretty light Ma favored.

"Yes, Josie."

We looked at each other, then turned our eyes to where we'd been digging. Honest, we sat there so long, the shadow from a pine tree inched toward us.

"What're we gonna do, Clementine?"

I got up, stiff, and my skirt wet from sitting in the snow. "We need Papa," I said.

Josie and I had marked the trail with two chunks of driftwood that we rolled up from the creek. Didn't want to lose Ma again. I was relieved to find Pa in front of the cabin chopping wood. When he saw me standing there out of breath, holding Ma's lantern, he dropped the ax.

"Where?" was all he said.

My sister and I stood off to the side while Pa and Tall Sing dug at the drift with their bare hands.

There was no sign of our mother. Pa was on his knees, sweeping his arm back and forth over the ground when he suddenly fell forward. As his shoulders started to disappear into a wide hole, Tall Sing quick sat on Pa's legs and pulled him to safety.

"Oh no," said my father.

I knew without him saying it. An old mine shaft. The boards crisscrossing the top were broken through. Ignoring Pa's protests, I got on my belly to look over the edge. It was dark except for something pale and crumpled on the bottom, maybe ten feet down. Ma's dress, I was certain.

"Mother?" I said.

Pa and Tall Sing took me by the arms and lifted me to my feet.

Don't know how folks heard or how many minutes passed, but now there were men gathering with ropes. I saw Jesse Blue lower himself into the pit, others standing by to pull him back up. Shorty was there and so was Whiskey Nose, his good arm around Josie, tears streaming into his beard. Puddin'head stood so close to my sister, she rested her hand on its back.

They brought Ma up at sunset. But for at least an hour the sky stayed light with pink and yellow clouds, like God was helping us see.

I reckoned Ma must've stepped off the trail for something

when she was following Pa that night before Christmas Eve. She knew the way to town and it had been a full moon, so maybe an animal had startled her into the trees. We would never know.

The men stood back as Pa, Josie, and I knelt beside my mother. She was cold as a block of ice, but oh, her face was pretty—some scratches, but she looked like she'd just gone to sleep. The pins from her hair had fallen out, so her golden braids hung down to her waist, like she must've worn them as a girl.

But when I saw her hands, my heart dropped. They were dark with dried blood and mud. Her fingernails were gone.

My stomach rolled with a sudden terror, a terror she must have felt. Her shock at falling, then not being able to climb out. How long had she screamed for help before it started snowing again and no one would be able to hear her? How long before she grew weary, then froze to death?

The thought of her last hours pierced me. I went numb; no tears came. But not so Josie. She laid her head across Ma's chest and cried her heart out.

As for Pa, he gasped like a man dying. "My fault!" he wailed over and over. His cries echoed off the canyon walls.

46
A Deal

Because my mother had been loved by so many, the miners in Nugget spent a goodly sum for dynamite to blast out a grave in the frozen cemetery. They did not want her to suffer the indignity of waiting until spring, stored in a cold shed. The murdered man remained there still. No one had been able to find out who he was.

During the funeral, Boone kept one arm around me, the other around Josie. Held us both real tight. Pa ran his hand over the wood coffin before it was lowered into the ground, then he hung his head and wept.

The next morning, Josie and I went back to cooking for the men. Boone came up the canyon to shovel the fresh snow off the roof and see to the firewood. He kept an eye on Pa, who was shivery and forlorn without whiskey. My father had finally sworn off drink. Hadn't touched a drop since we found Ma's lantern. After our customers left, I took Boone's hand and led him outside to our spot by the river.

When I told him about his father's scheme, his face twisted in disbelief. Then he pulled me to him so close I could feel the pounding of his heart. He said into my hair, "I'll kill 'im for this."

"No, Boone!"

Josie heard my cry and ran outside. When I told her about the deal, she began hurling stones into the water. Small ones at first, then bigger ones, fast and furious. I tried to put my arm around her, but she wrenched herself away.

"It ain't right, Clementine!" she yelled, running back into the house. She shoved the door closed with a loud thud.

Boone's eyes were brimming. "What will you do, darlin'?" he asked.

I did not answer.

That afternoon a boy on horseback brought a note from Judge Reno:

> *The rest of us must get on with living. Your swift response to my proposal is necessary, dear Clementine. Do not wait too long. LeRoy.*

LeRoy. Ma had taught me it meant "the king" in French. How I loathed that he had so much power over us. I wished Pa and Boone could figure out the tangled trap we were in without me having to do anything. I wanted to run away, taking my loved ones, and never look back.

But I could see only one way to save my family.

As I waited in the judge's small office, I looked out the window. Third Street was quiet, but just down the block the sidewalks on Main were busy with folks coming and going.

Melting snow made a river of mud in the center, with puddles big enough for wagons to get stuck.

"So you were saying . . ." Judge Reno returned to his desk with a piece of parchment. He dipped his quill in a jug of ink and began writing. "Continue," he said, without looking at me.

"Upon my agreeing to marry you," I went on, "per your suggestion and your promise, you will absolve my father, Dallas Kidd, of all debts, personal and otherwise. You will do everything in your considerable power to find him a job where he can earn an honest living. This contract is effective immediately, upon our signatures below."

Judge Reno kept writing, then blew on the ink for it to dry.

"I also would like three witnesses to sign with me," I said.

He raised his eyebrows. "Oh? Who?"

I thought of my mother's toughest, most loyal friends.

"Jesse Blue, Shorty, and Whiskey Nose," I said. They would raise a stink to high heaven if the judge didn't keep his end of the bargain.

"When?" he asked.

"Tomorrow morning. We'll all be here after I walk Josie to her classroom."

"No, dear," he said, with a laugh. "I mean our wedding. When may I have the pleasure of—?"

"Three days from now, when school's out," I interrupted, not wanting to hear what he meant by *pleasure*. "I want to be sure my sister is on her way to Boise, and I need to sew my bridal dress. Then I'll be able—"

Try as I might, I could not finish my sentence. I had just agreed to marry the man in front of me and I could not bring myself even to address him by name.

He didn't seem to notice. "You won't be sorry, Clementine. When I become governor of this fine territory, you'll be First Lady. I'll buy you all the pretty dresses you want."

I left my chair and got my coat. "Boone will never forgive you," I said. "Are you sure this is what you want? To lose him?"

The judge was no longer smiling.

47
Promises

The next morning, I took my time braiding my hair. Didn't wear it up pretty, like I did for Boone.

In Judge Reno's office, I signed my name at the bottom of the document. Plain and simple, no curlicues. He blotted his pen on a cloth, then signed with a flourish large enough to see from the across the room. When he came over and tried to kiss me, I put my hand on my lips before he could do so, and stepped away.

Whiskey Nose signed with his good hand, then Shorty and Jesse Blue.

I hurried out the door, but Shorty caught up to me on the front porch.

"Miss Clementine," he said, walking down the steps with me, "you don't ever have to worry about the judge not holdin' up his part." He opened the gate, then escorted me to Main Street.

I gave my friend a weak smile but didn't say anything.

"Anyhow," Shorty continued, "you probably already

know that the president of the United States ain't gonna appoint a man to be governor to this territory if he learns the fella has blood on his hands. In the eyes of the law, vigilantes ain't nothing more than murderers."

I looked at him, wondering what he meant.

"Yep," he said. "Me and the boys have made things real clear for the judge. He wants the governorship so bad, he'll be on his best behavior till kingdom come. It's a promise."

In the library, I was sorting new magazines and dime novels when I heard the door open and the sound of boots on the plank floor.

"May I help you?" I asked, turning.

There stood Boone in the small space by the counter. Gentle-like he closed the door and leaned against it. "I hope so," he answered.

I felt myself holding my breath.

"Clementine"—his voice was soft—"my father said you both signed papers this mornin'. So it's true?"

"It's true."

We stood in silence. Honest, I was heartsick. So many things I wanted to tell him.

Suddenly Boone rushed forward and clasped my arms. "I swear on my life I won't ever stop caring about you. Never."

I wiped my cheek with the back of my hand.

"Darlin', I'm leaving Nugget."

"*What?*"

"It'll be easier with some miles between us. You and my father being up here 'n all. I couldn't stand runnin' into you at the mercantile, knowin' you're his. I'd want to kill him with my bare hands."

"But where are you going?" I asked.

"There's lots of good acres down in the valley by Boise's river. I've always fancied planting an orchard. I've been saving money and I'll sell my cabin. It'll be enough to get me started."

I took a deep breath, trying to stay calm. Boone smelled so good—of fresh air and sunshine—that I wanted to rest my head on his shoulder and tell his despicable pa to forget everything. Tell *my* pa good-bye and good riddance. After all, he was the one who brought on his problems.

Boone ran his fingers over my braid, then turned me toward him. "Now I'm asking you for a favor, Clementine. If life don't work out between you and my pa, promise you'll send word. I'll come get you before the next sunset. You won't lack for one night without a roof over your head. You'll never lack for a thing."

I looked into his eyes, at the goodness I knew was missing in his father.

"I promise."

48
Closing Up Shop

The day before my wedding, I flurried about with a heavy heart.

Sewed myself a bridal veil from a lace curtain that had adorned our pantry window. Then attached it to a wreath for my hair. This I made from a thin branch of pine so on the morrow Josie and I could weave in fresh flowers. As for my gown, I decided to wear Ma's summer dress that had been in her trunk. It was pale yellow with blue and lavender embroidered around the neck and sleeves.

There also was packing for Josie. Not until she got to Mrs. Christianson's and looked through her things would she find where I had hidden her money. There was enough that she could pay for her whatnots for many years.

News about the Honorable Judge Reno marrying Clementine Kidd sent the ladies in town scurrying with preparations for a party, including scrubbing his house top to bottom.

The news shocked a lot of folks, especially Pa.

"I thought *Boone* was your sweetheart," he said, setting down his coffee to look at me.

We were on the sunny bench in front of our cabin. Lately, the temperature had been in the forties, warm enough to melt snow along the shore and hillsides. The river was running fast and was spilling over the banks, the most dangerous time of year.

"Papa, there's something you need to know." Then I told him about his debt being paid and why.

"It's a new start for you, Pa, a chance to honor Ma's memory and to be our good father again, but you got to give up your gambling and drinking for good. I'm not taking care of you anymore. I'll have my own life. If you want to be around for Josie and me, and to be a grandpa for our children, well, you got to pull yourself together."

It was a lot to say to my father in one breath, but time was short.

He looked at me with questions in his eyes, eyes that grieved for my mother. His unshaven cheeks were hollow from not eating. "Clementine, I'll be thanking you for the rest of my days."

Josie was still mad and throwing stones in the river every chance she got.

"I'm frettin' about you," she said to me while we were pouring pancake batter onto the griddle. It was to be the last meal we would serve for customers. Closing up shop is how we put it.

"Why can't we just work real hard to pay off Pa's debt?

Why? Then you wouldn't have to marry an old man you don't love. Oh, Clementine, Boone has had his heart set on you for such a long time."

I pulled a pan of sausages from the oven and set them on the table with the scrambled eggs. Then I took her hand.

"Josie, there're some things you won't understand for a while."

"How long is 'a while'?" She knocked away my hand. *"How long?"*

"Sooner than you think, honey."

My sister's eyes pleaded with me. "Clementine, I know you love Boone. I seen the way you look at him."

"Papa," I called, my voice shakier than I intended, "breakfast is ready!"

49

Wedding Gift

The next morning, Tall Sing brought Ma's dress back from a Chinatown laundry. It was wrapped in the prettiest red crinkle paper and smelled fresh from being hung out in the sun to dry. When I buttoned it up over my petticoat, it fit perfect.

After breakfast, I sat by the river with some wildflowers Josie had gathered for my wreath. Pa was restless, so he came over to see if there was anything he could do.

"My, aren't you the picture of your mother," he said. "I wish she was here. Can't believe our little girl is growed up."

"Oh, Papa." I handed him a spool of thread. "Here. Use this to wrap around the flower stem, then tie it on like so."

After three daisies he said, "Oh, before I forget." Setting down the spool, he leaned to the side to take something from his pocket. Out came a small wooden box, which he handed to me. "Here you go, darlin'. I gave this to your ma on our weddin' day. Reckon she'd want you to wear it on yours."

I moved the flowers aside, then opened the lid. Nestled

on a scrap of gingham was the prettiest brooch I ever saw: a flower the size of a silver dollar with a ruby in its center. "Oh, Papa, it's beautiful."

"Yep. Had it made there in Californie, jeweler was a friend of ours."

I looked up at Pa. "I've never seen this before. How come Ma never wore it?"

"Well, it was like this. She used to wear it when we were young and went dancin' in town, but the other ladies made remarks about her being rich and so forth. Finally your ma tucked it away in a safe place so folks wouldn't think she was puttin' on airs."

Careful, I lifted it from the box and held it up to the sunlight. The silver sparkled and the jewel was a deep red. Turning it over, I saw Pa's inscription:

To my beloved wife,
Annabelle Ruby June Kidd.
3 August 1849

"It surely is a work of art," I said. Then I thought of something. All the rampages Pa had gone on to find cash, he had left Ma's treasure alone. "You could've sold this, Pa, when you needed money. How come you didn't? Ma never would've known."

"Ho! Clementine, she would've knowed sure as I'm sitting on this bench. Yes, she would've."

I squinted into the sun to look at him.

"My word, yes," he said. "For years and years, every single

night before we went to bed, she took out the box and opened the lid for a long look. *Dallas Kidd,* she'd say, *it's still pretty as ever.* Even nights I came home late, she looked at it. Would tell me so the next morning. Clementine, crazy fool that I've been, I wouldn't've taken away her weddin' brooch. Never."

He gazed out at the river and drew in a deep breath.

After some moments I said, "Weddin's set for noon, Papa, in the chapel just down from the canyon."

He patted my hand, then stood up. "I'll be there, darlin'. Gonna go visit that barber first."

PART III

Josie, Two Years Later

Boise City

Territory of Idaho

Spring 1869

50
At Mrs. Christianson's

"Josie?" someone was sayin' through my dream. "Josie, wake up, it's your birthday, remember?"

I opened my eyes and there was Libby starin' down at me, her red hair a mess of curls. She was eight years old and didn't fancy a brush or ribbons like other girls. "There's a surprise downstairs for you," she said, now seein' that I was awake.

"All right, I'm a-comin'." I felt hungry from the good cookin' smells of ham and fried potatoes driftin' up the stairway, and quick got dressed.

I followed Libby downstairs, she jumpin' two steps at a time, me more ladylike—one step, then another, on account I was now thirteen years of age. First off, I hugged Tall Sing where he stood at the stove. Then I threw my arms around Mrs. Christianson, who was as plump as a pretty hen.

"Why, there you are, dear," she said. "And happy birthday! Josie, have a look over there on the parlor table. A fella from the post office brought a package for you just after sunup."

I looked at Tall Sing, wonderin' if he knew who it was from. He was crackin' eggs into the big stirrin' pan and glanced at me sideways, but did not say a word.

The parcel was small enough to fit in my hand, wrapped in brown paper and glued on the ends. It wouldn't be from Pa, on account he was comin' for supper and didn't need to mail me anythin'. I stared at the postmark.

"Open it, open it!" Libby said, squirmy like always. It had taken me only five minutes to figure out why her mama needed someone to help take care of her, what with her papa dead and gone. "The Tomato Tornado" is what the gardener called her when he thought no one was listenin'.

"I'm gonna open it upstairs, Libby Lou. You stay here and help Tall Sing."

My quilt was heavy from all the coins Clementine had sewed into the hem. I reckoned if our windows were open durin' a storm, it would not blow off my bed, it was that heavy. Funny thing was, I didn't even need one nickel on account of Mrs. Christianson was treatin' me like a daughter. She made sure I wanted for nothin'.

Also, Pa was givin' me a coin now and then. He lived upstairs at the Boise Mercantile, where his job there was keepin' him plenty busy. And for two years now he had stayed away from the poker tables. And the whiskey.

But I am off the subject.

Package in hand, I sat in the window seat that looked out over the gardens and the carriage house. Tall Sing had his own room there, above the stable, where he kept his medicines and such. All along the picket fence and porch, the honeysuckle vines were in bloom. The scent of their perfume comin' through our open windows made me glad to be alive.

Careful, I peeled the paper away from a wooden box, then wiggled off the lid.

"*Oh.*" My breath came quick and quicker.

It was Ma's brooch, the silver flower with a ruby in the center. The one Clementine wore on her weddin' day.

My eyes went blurry. When I saw the letter, I picked it up and held it to my heart.

51
The Letter

I unfolded the cream-colored stationery. Printed up top in blue was this address:

Woman's Medical College of Pennsylvania
229 Arch Street
Philadelphia, Pennsylvania

Quick, my eyes went to the bottom of the page, to the signature, then I smiled.

"It's about time," I whispered.

I closed my eyes. A breeze was fluffin' the curtain over my knees. I could hear horses cloppin' along the dirt road and the shouts of some boys playin' with a dog that barked and barked. All was regular. I counted to three, then began readin'.

Dearest Josie,
As promised two years ago, I am sending you
Ma's brooch to celebrate that I have at long last

finished my schooling and am about to take exams. By the time you are reading these words, I'll already be on the train bound for Laramie and as far west as it goes, then on a stage to Fort Boise. With me will be my Certificate of Medicine and your many letters that I have read countless times.

In Mrs. Christianson's last note, she offered me a room until I find a place to hang my shingle. Did you know that Pa already writes to me as "Doc Clementine"? And Boone starts his letters, "Dear Miss True Shot," though I haven't held a rifle in all these months.

Must close now. The girls and I are about to take a stroll by the harbor. A ship from England is making her way upriver and will dock within the hour—I wish you could see her tall white sails!

My love to you, Josie, as the dogwoods are blooming!

Your adoring sister, Clementine

I pinned Ma's brooch onto my doll's dress, the doll Pa had given me when I was ten. Then I unbuttoned the hem of her double petticoat that I had sewn into a large pocket—no one but me knew about it, not even Libby. She had her own shelves of dolls and toys. Anyhow, inside the pocket was one newspaper story and Clementine's letters. I uncrinkled them to read in order, like always.

The first one was from the terrible day after she was s'posed to get married. In the stagecoach goin' down the mountain away from Nugget, Tall Sing handed it to me.

It was written in my sister's hand, but there were only six words:

The river brings life, not death.

Tall Sing leaned close so I could hear him. "Think, Josie."

My eyes were still wet that morning and I had hiccups. As our coach swayed and jangled on the downhill trail, the other passengers kept givin' me sympathetic looks. Everyone in Nugget knew how Ma died, and that my sister drowned on her weddin' day.

"Honey, everything'll be all right," said the lady across from me, offerin' her lace hankie for my nose.

A man in buckskins agreed with her. "We're awful sorry for your tragedy, little girl. Life just ain't fair sometimes."

Tall Sing touched his finger to his lips so I wouldn't get to talkin'. He looked in my eyes like he wanted me to think about those six words from Clementine.

And I *was* thinkin'. I pondered what she meant about the river. We had found her bridal wreath on our footbridge, but that's all. Nothin' washed up on shore anywhere. Not her shoes, no scrap of dress, no body.

All of a sudden my hiccups stopped. I grabbed Tall Sing's arm so I could whisper in his ear. "Is Clementine . . . Is she still . . . ?"

Quick, he put his hand on mine, nodding, then he stared out the window that was cut into the door. Right then I knew to keep quiet. We were on the worst seat—facin' forward—so all the dust was blowin' on us, makin' my eyes sting. I used

202

the lady's hankie to cover my face. Did not want anyone to see that my tears had turned to a smile.

That first night in my new home—after Libby was tucked in bed—Tall Sing explained to me and Mrs. Christianson the secret we must keep. He would tell Pa and Boone the next day, when they came to Boise to make sure I was settled.

Just the five of us were to know. At least for the time bein'.

So the days and weeks of my new life began by me stayin' busy with Libby Lou. And waitin' to hear from my sister.

52
To No One's Regret

"Breakfast is hot 'n ready, Josie. Come on down!" Libby hollered from the bottom of the stairs.

"I'm a-comin'!"

"Did you open your package yet?" she shouted.

"Tell you later!"

As I tucked away the letters, I unfolded the newspaper story to read for the hundredth time. It was short and sweet, just how I like 'em.

Judge LeRoy H. Reno Killed in
Gunfight Up Cougar Canyon

Boone had been the only one that paused at this news. By then he was livin' near us in Boise City, plantin' his orchard. He took off his hat for a moment to think about things, then back on it went to shade his sunburned face. He went to pushin' his wheelbarrow across the field, just like regular. It was the first time I heard Boone a-whistlin'.

The gun fight happened one month after his pa was s'posed to marry Clementine. That dirty ol' judge already had got himself a girlfriend—Miss Mabel from Lucky Jim's Saloon. But we heard that Miss Mabel didn't go to his funeral either.

Everyone was sayin' that Judge Reno passed away to no one's regret.

After Libby and I cleaned up the breakfast pans, I went to my room. On account that it was my birthday, Mrs. Christianson was mostly excusin' me from my chores. And I felt like gettin' fancy.

I put on my best dress, the one Mrs. Christianson had sewed for my church-goin'. It had a high lace collar with a little flounce over my behind. Then, just for fun, I brushed my hair into four braids, tied the ends with ribbons, and went downstairs.

Mrs. Christianson was on the back porch arrangin' flowers for the bouquet that was always on our table. Libby was jumpin' rope by the water pump, barefoot, and splashin' mud on herself. They looked at me as I came down the steps.

"Where you off to, sweetheart?" asked Mrs. Christianson. "My, how lovely you look."

"Boone's Apple Orchard. I've got an important message to deliver," I answered.

She smiled, knowin' exactly what I was talkin' about.

Libby threw her rope down. "Can I go, too?"

"Yes, Libby Lou. But get you some shoes on. There's lots of stickers in the dirt."

Meantime, I looked over at Tall Sing sittin' in the porch rocker. He was readin' a book. His long pigtail hung down through the arm slats, and directly below him was my yellow kitty, battin' at the soft tip of his hair.

Tall Sing and I smiled at each other. Then he went back to readin'.

Author's Note

When I was a kid at Girl Scout camp my friends and I learned a bunch of folksongs, among them "Oh My Darling Clementine!" which we belted out with gusto. Now, some decades later, I thought it would be fun to connect this old favorite with a work of historical fiction; thus, this novel.

It is thought that Percy Montross composed the original music and lyrics in the early 1880s, and that he based this song on "Down by the River Liv'd a Maiden" by H.S. Thompson (1863). Since then, "Clementine" has become popular with several different stanzas that children sing in school, Scouts, and around summer campfires.

A final note: The Woman's Medical College of Pennsylvania was chartered and opened in 1850 as the Female Medical College of Pennsylvania. It was in Philadelphia and was the first medical school in the world for women. It offered homeopathic studies with joint MD and HMD degrees.

I would like to thank the diligent editorial team at Holiday House, especially my editor, Leanna Petronella, for her patience and good judgement, and for her sense of fun.

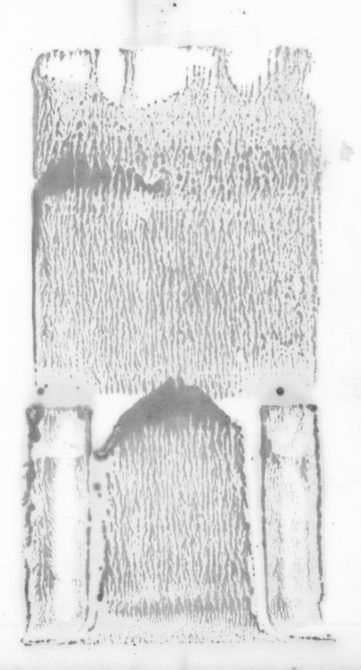

I AND THOU